OAKEN TONGUE

L. MORTON

OAKEN TONGUE

TALES OF RETURNING TO NATURE

L. MORTON

ISBN: 9798376783887

Cover illustration by Thomas Morton
Interior illustrations by Ali Eroglu and Sarah Ganly

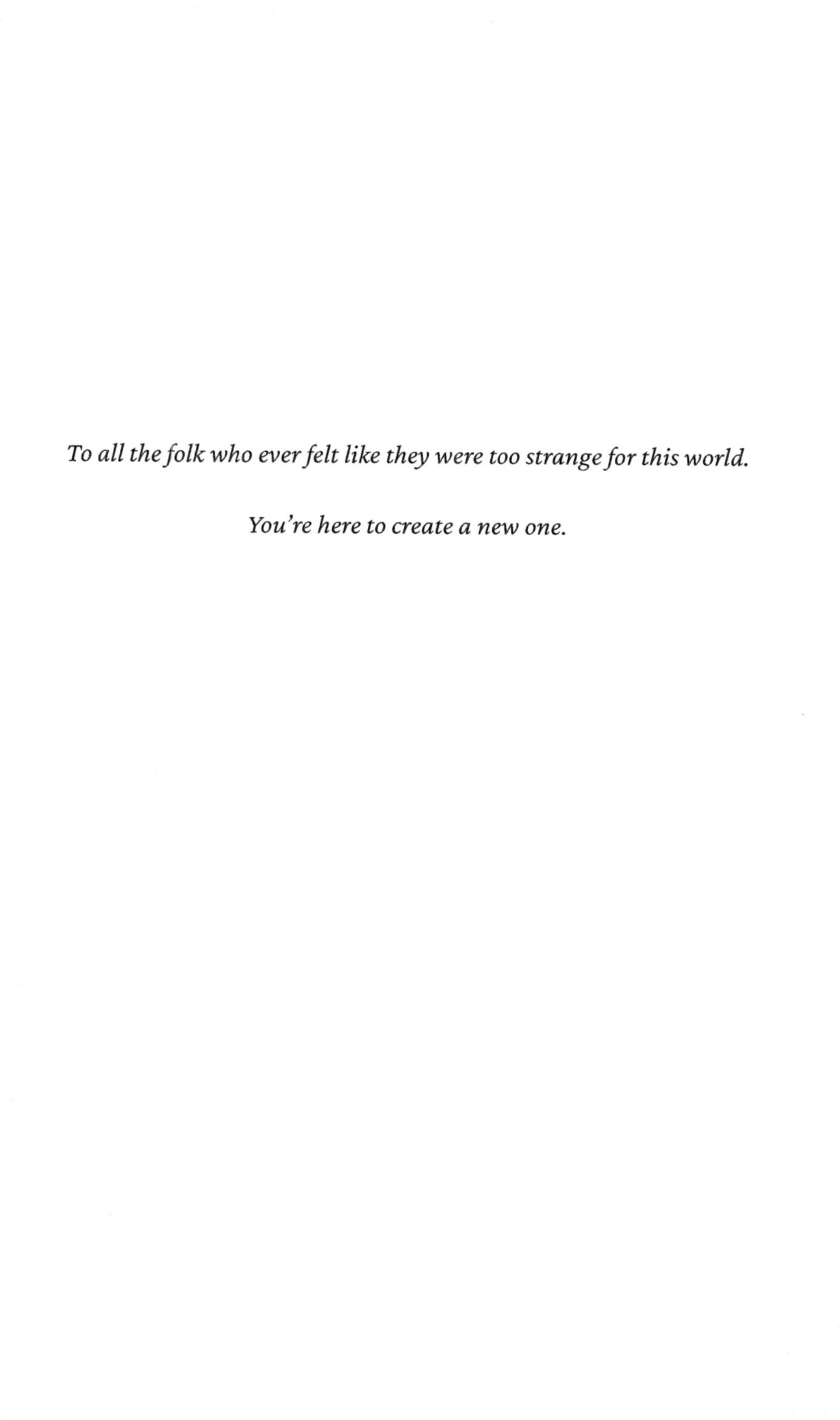

To all the folk who ever felt like they were too strange for this world.

You're here to create a new one.

CONTENTS

BEGINNINGS

Tell me, reader, have you ventured down into the dark places? You know the places I speak of.

For there are cities that fold on the edge of seasons and secrets that can be found only in the in-between time when the summer king hands over his crown to autumn's deathly kiss. These are places where the drip of cavern walls promise a lullaby and even the earth's mulch has a tale to tell in its quiet decay.

Tell me, reader, do you still knock on the doors of great oak trees and giggle with their freshly fallen acorns when no one is watching? Have you made fool-hardy promises to the fae queen lately and run from her impatient shadows at the edge of morning's dew?

Have you set your head against the mud and softened your gaze, looking out at the worlds between blades of grass, listening all the while for those lingering spaces unspoken between words?

I know you have.

Tell me, reader, does it frighten you to think awhile upon death and her blackened eyes? Do you pull the curtains closed when you feel the cold breath against your window and turn your head to other things when you hear that old familiar knocking at the door?

Nature is a true neutral. Consider the soft lilac of a springtime flower and the gentle sunlight on your face as you lap at the sweet juice of the berry bush. Now consider the young bodies unrotten in the pit of the bog, the bite of frost upon the mountainside and the hare bones strewn across the moor. Nature does not differentiate, she is not cruel, and she is not kind. She is nothing more and nothing less than herself, which is neither and both, reflecting the duality within us all.

The writings in Oaken Tongue are not intended as tales of horror or negativity, although at first glance, some of them could seem that way. Each story and poem is imbued with the magic of traditional folklore and mythology and focuses on the theme of returning to nature in all of her forms.

I always was a storyteller, and I gravitated towards those tales of faraway lands, of shapeshifters and badly behaved women. The stories that left you wondering, shaken, and thirsting for adventure.

And so, those are the stories I intend to share with you in this volume. Warnings of just what can happen when we reject our true nature, when we hide ourselves away and refuse to step into our power. There are tales of madness and ignorance wrought with vengeance, but also of light, beauty, and power. Tales of being true to ourselves, of loving ourselves as we are, and of what can be achieved through deep reverence and communion with nature.

May they guide you, awaken some dusty truths you had hidden away, slightly disturb you, and most of all, *inspire you.*

I
FANG AND FUR

It was just the wolves and I in those days, but that was the way I wanted it.

Wolf Mother had found me as a half-starved babe, lying silent against the roots of the ancient oak. My flesh was soft as lilac petals, and no fur swaddled me in its wildness and warmth, and so I trembled as I lay there dying, bidding farewell to my short life on this earth. My bones had brittled from malnourishment, and the bluish veins that tracked my arms struggled to carry the weary blood through my fragile form. I don't remember much from those days, save the drowning dreams of ice water flooding my lungs and dark eyes staring down at me, ever watching. Wolf Mother had seen others like me, she said. Infants with stumps where limbs should be, glassy eyes that could not sense the light and dark above them, or those with facial features disfigured and mangled, much like my own. Each child had been left under the great oak tree, where their wails soon faded into the leaf mulch, their bones becoming still as rigor took them. After a while, she said, the worms came to suckle on their sinew and the crows picked at them noisily, arguing among themselves for each ill-gotten morsel. She told me of the bickering with disgust in her feral eyes. Dirty creatures, crows are, eating rot and meat that has gone bad and laughing all the while.

When she first scented me in the early hours of the fragile morn, she thought I was prey, and stalked in silence until she cast her wolfish eyes upon my form. She believed me to be dead like the others, but as she turned to leave, she glimpsed the slightest twitch of my near-frostbitten toe as I struggled against the goddess of death. My face was unlike the others from my pack, she told me, it was missing parts. The space around my jaw had developed malformed and wrong. I tested my tongue in my mouth and pushed my mangled lips together, but try as I might, I could not howl aloud as she could. Instead, I lay silent upon the sodden earth and did not cry in the way the babes before me had. Not long from birthing her own litter, she pitied the cub in me, I think, and carried me back to the den where her children snoozed softly, snouts curled into their tails. In the early days, their black eyes scanned me with suspicion, for I did not look as they did. Close to death, I could not help their pack, instead I would take the attention of their mother. But Wolf Mother hushed them and told them I was pack now, and slowly, they began to accept me.

I believe I did see death one night. The ache in my bones was too much for my feeble form, and I wished more than once that everything would end, that she would take me. Robed in ivory and crowned in autumn leaves, she visited me in a dream and looked upon me fondly. I wished to follow her, and she told me it was likely she'd come for me the following night, but Wolf Mother brought me back. I suckled at her teat with her cubs, and the nectarous milk nourished my rattling bones.

In those days, I was small enough to lie with her, buried in the safety of musk and fur as she curled up to slumber. Nestled in that grey haven smelling of wild places and clean air, strength came to me gently as a stranger would approach. My limbs grew longer, and I tried them on for size. First, they trembled beneath me, but I watched the muscle ripple on my brothers and sisters as they ran, and an aching filled me, so each day I stood upon them and willed my gangly legs forward. It wasn't long until I was able to follow the cubs on their hunts and watch them as they each made their first kill. I did not possess the tools of fang and jaw in the way that they did, but still, I ran with them as fast as I could. Often, I was last, often I fell, and often I failed in my hunt. But still I ran, and I did not complain. And in this way, they accepted me.

We watched the sunrise yawn and collapse into eventide, and I ran with my brothers and sisters, the knife-edged thrill of the hunt surging through my malformed bones. I feasted on the flesh of hare and tore at sinew with my stubby fingers, feeling the tang of hot blood in my mouth until I was satiated. The hunt strengthened me, and I grew in health and agility, but still, I could not make a sound. My siblings howled to the swollen moon, they growled in jest and yapped at one another, but no voice had I. The hunt was not all we lived for. Often, we played, and would run in circles until one of us was pinned to the dew-dappled grass, a tangle of limbs both hairless and not. There they were, all wild eyes and bone and teeth, pounding with the energy of youth and ready for anything. And so was I.

I do believe those were the best days of my life.

But years pass in the blink of a lash, and soon Wolf Mother wore silver hairs at her snout, and her bones began to ache. She could no longer join us on the hunt and wearied more often, so my brothers and sisters brought her rabbit flesh as she rested her head in the den. I lay with her often then, as I had when I was a babe, but this time I curled myself around her and warmed her as her teeth chattered even during summer's blessing. I grasped that grey fur in my hands and breathed deeply the scent of her wild ways. Oh, Wolf Mother, my saviour. One morning, when dew studded the grass spears and summer's haze blossomed over the hillsides, warming the moors with his molten gaze, she declared that she felt better and ventured from the den. The sunrise licked the horizon, and the air was warm already as she stretched and yawned beneath it all. She said that it would be a beautiful day, and we would find good hunting and a clear sky with a silver moon that night.

And then suddenly, she lay down and died.

And we did not mourn her, for that was the way of all things.

To live was to die, and she passed from this world and joined the dead things as they burrowed in the earth. I watched as her flesh fell from the bone and collapsed into the soil. I let the worms feed on her and make the earth rich and fecund, but the crows, I pushed away, baring my teeth. She would not have liked them. My brother led us after that, and many of my siblings found a mate and bore cubs of their own. We enjoyed many years of peace together underneath those unfurling sunrises, so generous with their light. Those long days of summer were like a fresh kill to me, satiating and blanketed in contentment, so I stretched out beneath the old oak tree where I had begun my life and let it wash over me like golden honeycomb. I snoozed awhile and dreamt of running across moorland, the snap of fox bone and the sound the heather made as it bent in the feral breeze. I was torn from my peace by a strange squawking unlike any bird I had heard before, and when I opened my eyes, two creatures stood over me. They were tall, and although they had no fur of their own, they were draped in animal skins and carried strange objects with them. They stared down at me and there was something in their eyes I recognised, the same glint I saw in the eyes of the prey. Could it be fear that they carried within them?

They squawked among themselves awhile and one pulled off the animal skin he wore, draping it across me. I sniffed it. It was warm, but I did not recognise the scent, and it did not feel safe. I shrugged it off in alarm, but the male reached down and set his hands upon my neck. Panic flooded through me, and I writhed, breath ragged, but he tied the animal skin so it stayed in place, then he let me go. Something of him triggered ancient memories in me, but I could not place them. He crouched before me and spoke in warbles, I did not know what he was trying to tell me, and I did not want to know. He looked disappointed, the way my brother's eyes rounded and darted downwards towards the earth when a hunt had been unsuccessful. He set his hand upon my arm, urging me to stand on two limbs. The feel of his flesh on mine sent shivers through my form, and I did not want to stand with him. I tried to tell him this, to explain it all, but I could not make a noise.

I quivered in the most peculiar way, the standing upon two legs unfamiliar to me. What did they want? They chattered to one another in that warbling fashion and shook their heads, I think they were sad. I glanced over my shoulder, concerned now, where was my pack? They slept in the den, I thought, and I wished now more than ever that I could howl for them. I wanted these men to leave me alone, but they tugged at me, and I sensed they wished me to follow. I pulled away and curled my lips in a snarl, baring my teeth. They looked at one another and tightened their grip, pulling me with them. I was scared then, and I did not wish to go. But I felt dizzy and afraid, and my breath caught in my throat as everything faded into darkness under a midnight sky of midday. I thought then that the goddess of death had finally come for me, and I had departed to join Wolf Mother, but it was still not yet my time.

When I awoke from my dizzy dreams of dew-drunkenness and hare blood, I found they had carried me to their den. I lay upon a strange nest and sniffed at the layers that swaddled me. I recognised this scent, it was made of sheep. The skins itched as I writhed and I felt a smothering heat rise within me, so I cast them off my body, panting. Where was I? The den appeared to be built from rocks, but strange colours like summer flower petals coated the walls. There were peculiar objects fashioned from ash and oak, and orange heat crackled lurid in the corner. One hundred other scents flooded my senses, and not one of them did I recognise. Fear had begun to take me, but I thought of Wolf Mother and my siblings, and the cower of rabbits beneath their stare. I am not prey; I am a hunter. I steeled myself.

A hole appeared in the wall and a female of their pack came towards me, her new-born doe eyes glassy and afraid. She moved towards me slowly, her approach uncertain and cautious, then she curved her lips upwards and rested a hand on my arm. It was warm and gentler than the men, but I still felt my heartbeat quicken and a desire to pull away. The woman reached into water and carried something towards me. At first, I thought it was more sheep skin, but it was a texture I did not recognise, soft and damp. I recoiled from the touch at first, but as she dragged it over my skin, I decided to let her do it. The dirt on my arms came away and left my fleshy skin exposed underneath. This went on for a while, and when I was finally dirtless, she put her hands upon my head, and ran her fingers over my coat, shaking her head sadly. I looked at her own coat, golden like honey, cascading past her shoulders like stream water. Healthy and well fed. I looked to my own and saw the mass of bark-brown hair falling from my head, it was matted and solid. As her hand ran over it, I felt a strange feeling I did not recognise. Although no injury had I, it hurt me to look towards her golden curls, and I wanted to run back to my den and hide. She curved her lips to me again and began to pull a piece of beech bark carved into fangs through my coat. It tugged at my head, and I snarled at her, so she drew away, afraid, and it was a while before she came back.

But she did come back. She worked at my coat for a long time, and I was fed up with the snagging, but I did not snarl again. Something in those watery eyes made me not want to. When it was loose and free, she poured water upon it, and I scented rose petals. I let her do it, and when she was done, she looped it in a way that was unfamiliar to me and tied it at the ends. I felt it smooth against my shoulder, and the dark feeling in the pit of my belly began to subside. But this was not my home, and I wanted to ask her where my pack was, to tell her I had to return, but I could not speak. People came and went after that. They all looked at me with their brows furrowed and spoke in those warbled noises over me, endlessly squawking and squabbling. Tall men prodded at me and hurt me with their strange devices, and ever I felt a prickling of my heckles in their vivid presence. The woman shook her head at them and placed her hands on me gently. I knew the look in her eyes, she wanted me like fresh prey, and she wanted to keep me for herself. She changed my furs and draped me in layers the colour of petals, her eyes sparkling and cheeks flushing as she tied fabrics upon my head and ran her wood-fangs through my coat. I did not know why. I tried to whine at night, I think. I wanted to see my brothers and sisters, and I thought often of Wolf Mother. Hunger gnawed at my belly, and when they brought me strange things to eat, I could no longer turn my head from them. It smelled like meat I did not recognise, and it was warm, though not with blood and life, but from the orange heat that crackled in the corner.

The seasons collapsed into one another, and the light outside began to fade. Cold crept in at the edges of the den, and even my heart mirrored the frost with its darkened chill. The woman took me outside now, and my soul ached at the scent of winter pine and the snow-soaked freedom promised in the forest ahead. I considered running from her many times, but each time I thought of the strange men and stayed with her. She looped her arm in mine and bundled me in furs as I walked with her around their dens. So many of them in one place. They stood behind piles of fish and sheep's wool and shouted in that warbling manner. I did not know why, but it made her face light up. The man behind the fish did not like me, I could tell. I knew his expression and its meaning by now, he thought me sickly and malformed, but his hatred had metamorphosed into fear. I had babe-wrought memories of this rejection. I asked the woman if I could return to the forest, but she did not understand and stared at me puzzled.

Something in my mouth had grown wrong, and I could not get a sound out.

At spring's first kiss, she began to let me walk alone. Many moon cycles had passed us overhead now, and I saw her trust grow in me. I often saw smaller folk who looked more like me, and though I was grown to my family, I wondered if I was still a cub here. I walked the cluster of dens with a gnawing in my bones; a writhing, unsatiated need to leave this place. Darkness cloaked the earth when the fish man came to me, opening his soft mouth wide and hooting to the night sky. I did not like it. He prodded me and pushed me to the floor, kicking me as I lay quaking. I was hurt and tried to howl, to tell my woman, but I could not. But from the floor I could run like a wolf again, and I pushed my limbs before me and leapt as fast as I could. He wanted me to die, I knew it. He did not like my strangeness, the way my body had grown wrong, the way my woman doted on me. He came to me now and held me down, squeezing his hands to my throat so that I could not breathe. I thrashed and writhed and thought of how the rabbits fought when we hunted them.

But he was not a hunter, and I was not prey.

I kicked and bit, the adrenaline rushing through my body as I thought of my brother and the uncontainable way he hunted. I copied the angle of his jaw, the pouncing of his legs, and I found my teeth to be sharp, sharp enough to draw blood and cause the man to fall back in alarm. Air rushed into my lungs and heat flooded my body once more. In a blooded haze of wolves and wild things, my body followed its instincts and leapt upon the man. I felt his dirty hands grasp at me, but I ripped into his skin with no remorse or doubts. And so, I tore him to shreds. I ripped his flesh from its bones and feasted on the gore like he was a river rat. Sinew tangled in my teeth as I dined on his carcass, and I felt the thrill of the hunt take a place inside me. When I was finished, I ran deeper into the woods. I followed the scent of wild places and raven feathers, and I ran all night until I reached the great oak tree at morning's first light. I listened for the soft howl of my brother and heard it on the wind, I would soon be home. I thought back to the kill I had left at the edge of the woods, of blood and bone and dead things.

And I did not feel anything.

For I was a wolf, and wolves do not mourn.

LUNGS OF THE STORM
BONES OF THE EARTH

2

REBIRTH

I first noticed it on the eve of a particularly warm Friday in midsummer. The swollen sun moved lower in the sky and began to filter through the blooming trees, spreading his molten tendrils across the fields and yawning as his gangly limbs began the nightly descent into their bed of ink.

It started as a mere prickling of the skin, a gentle breeze that spread its way across my arms, unusually cool for the thick mugginess of July. The hairs on my body began to rise as that peculiar wind pushed its way into my rotting lungs, causing the air inside my very body to tingle and expand. But I pushed it to the side as the sun bid me farewell, blinking it away between heavy spider lashes and smoothing the hairs on my arms back down. I shook my head and almost laughed at how silly I had been. How fanciful.

I returned to the office the following Monday like I had every Monday before that, folding starch-crackled fabric around my sickly body and pulling a noose-tie around my throat as I spluttered on the black tar of another day. I smiled at my neighbour who stood at the bus stop and remarked on how beautiful a morning it was as my blank eyes looked out across the concrete. I felt them droop and glaze over with a film of river sludge as I watched the bus rattle its way towards me, but still, I felt nothing. I shuffled my papers and asked my colleagues about their weekends and made sure I stayed late to feel the hum of electricity burrow itself into the recesses of my brain, my eyes yellowing at the glare of the screens. By the end of the day, I had almost forgotten that strange breeze.

I did not feel it again until a month later.

It began the same way, with a rush of cold air and the uncertainty of a new-born lamb quivering as it pushed itself up on its spindle-legs for the very first time. I was standing at the bus stop again in the early hours of a Tuesday morning and the sickly glow of the toiling sunrise was weaving its way above the concrete when the glistening of a silver web caught my eye. I noticed her sitting there watching me, her black limbs seeming to wave in a way that beckoned me into the very web itself. In a second of fancy, I rushed towards the bus shelter and pressed my nose against the glass, staring out through her creation as my rotting breath spread its vapours across the mould-crusted surface. My neighbour cleared her throat as the bus pulled up and the great hiss of the engine drawing to a jittery halt snapped me out of my stupor. I chuckled and glanced at the beady eyes of the others, and they smiled nervously back at me. How silly I was being.

I sat at my desk and stared into the void of the sizzling screen, but I couldn't settle for some reason. I picked at my fish-grey sandwich with dirty fingernails and cast it into the bin to join the other flotsam. I felt a prickle run over my skin, perhaps I was becoming unwell. When asked about the weather I only smiled, staring out of the window at the grey brick beyond, half hoping for the glistening of her web. They asked me to stay late but I told them I felt nauseous, I didn't know what it was, but something unnatural writhed in the pit of my stomach. Beads of sweat began to form on my overheated flesh as I broke out in trembles under the glare of the UV lights. I told them of my headache and began to babble in a secret language I had not spoken before. I saw their empty eyes dart towards each other, disapproving and concerned.

They were onto me, I knew it. I could sense their conniving mutterings behind my back. My head snapped over my shoulders as I glanced behind me in fear, concerned for what may dwell there. They were conspiring against me; I knew this now. I could feel the whispers pressing into my skin and the shuffling of letters slicing paper cuts into my soft body. Bile sizzled in my stomach, and I ran to the bathroom, heaving on all fours like a beast, and yet nothing came.

That night I was restless. The blistering heat made it impossible to get comfortable, but the fan blowing cool air into my room tickled the hair on my legs and caused me to writhe like hungry maggot children beneath the magnolia soap dust of the suffocating sheets. I felt every breath within me struggle to make its way down to my aching lungs as I coughed and spluttered, the sickness growing and spreading throughout my body. The very sinew of my muscles quivered, and I felt my head racing with thoughts that were not mine, memories I didn't recognise. That was when I looked up at the ceiling and saw her in the corner.

Her.

That web once so graceful was now heavy with tomb-dust and cobwebbed in the recesses of my bedroom. Sickly and yellowing, the paint peeled from the ceiling and revealed rotten wood beneath it, overflowing with rat tails. The very colour of the walls caused me to tremble, even the furniture seemed to undulate in a grotesque manner as if to mock me. I looked up at her, still and silent in the corner, was she laughing at me too? I blinked and she was gone, but a voice drifted in from the open window. An otherworldly voice that made the very air constrict in my raw throat. A voice made of both shadow and light. A voice that flowed with the grace of a stream and yet grumbled like soil spilling from a cave's gaping mouth. I did not recognise the language, but I understood its meaning. I felt a tug somewhere deep between the folds of my organs and moved to the window, throwing it open and tasting the acrid scent of summer magics. I stuck my head out into the night air and shouted to the tar-like sky, begging it to stop this inane babble!

All at once, my bowed legs carried me from the house and I stood there, naked in the garden, howling to the sky as I collapsed to the earth, tearing the perfectly manicured grass up between my knuckles and sobbing. I saw lights appear in windows and the shuffling of my neighbour's curtains, but I could do nothing but wail. My eyes locked onto the glisten of her web beneath my feet, this time it weaved its way across the garden path into the street, so I began to run. My bare feet shattered against the concrete as I made contact with the crumbling rock, following the tendrils of her web until I reached the edge of the forest.

The moon looked down at my pain and smiled serenely, she had seen this before. She sighed gently and with her exhale, soft silver light covered my naked body, illuminating my path into the trees. I dropped to my knees and crawled on all fours through the undergrowth, mud clawing beneath my fingernails and my bare flesh scraping along the bracken. I welcomed the joyous sting as it tore my skin and drew blood, dripping my wounds into the dead wood as I moaned and sang heathen worship to the fangs of the thorns.

I came to a clearing and I found myself suddenly unafraid. I threw back my stupid head and howled secret mysteries into the blackened sky. All manner of strange creatures began to crawl out from under the blackberry bushes and watch me, unconcerned. I saw the stripe of the badger and the fire of fox tail as their eyes stared out at me from between the leaves.

Tiny bodies covered in ivy with limbs like willow pushed up from the mud, expressionless as I shrieked and tore at my hair, pulling the strands from my scalp and arranging them into strange symbols on the earth. The fox threw his head back and screamed along with me, cackling into the darkness as the others began to steadily join in. Insects screamed and tittered in the bushes, a cacophony of yearning and belonging.

Then all at once, they fell silent.

I began to laugh.

A belly laugh so deep that even the trees chuckled with me. I felt their roots dancing beneath me as if they had been tickled by moonlight herself. I lay on my belly in the dirt and kissed the dense mud, tasting the fertility of the wet ground and exhaling fully for the first time in my life. A release, a joy, a belonging. I felt my limbs begin to crack and harden, forming swirling bark-skin as tiny buds burst forth from my fingertips. Soil filled my mouth and spilled from the abyss of my eyes as I plunged into the earth and worms feasted on my flesh. I watched myself from afar and basked in the glorious serenity of it all.

I was home. I was finally home.

3

BOG BODIES

There was a time when my mouth was not full of mud. Yes, from these now mire-blackened teeth I once whispered kind words to children, crooned worship to the flies and cackled so loud it shook sparrows from the very treetops. From this grit-caked tongue I lapped the juice of autumn's last blackberries and tasted the sweet cream of cows giddy on spring's love song. With these lips of rot and putrid places, I peppered soft kisses on milky skin and sipped at teacups brimming with rose petals.

But I am getting ahead of myself, now, so I shall tell you the tale.

So, as I said, there was a time when my mouth was not full of mud.

I those days I wandered through the forest in summer rain, my empty mouth giddy and hopeful. A young creature, I was, dark eyes alight with youth and the promise of warm days stretching endlessly on. My mother and father died from the sickness when I was young, so I took over the tending of our home. I think it was then... yes, it was then, that I decided I wanted to become a healer. I watched them as a young child, their frail greening bodies blanketed in black boils, the sweetness in the air so foul I could not stand it. I fed them watery soup straight from the ladle and set a damp cloth upon their foreheads as they choked and spluttered up dark vomit. The sickness spread from the south and wound its way around the village, creeping in through cracks in doorways and spreading like flies on a rotting heap.

My father went first, his death rattle quaking the foundations and splintering the thatched roof as his bones crumbled underneath him. My mother was not far off then. If heartbreak makes an audible crack I know I heard hers shatter, and she died hand in hand with him, infected tears streaking her yellowed skin. I ran from the house and brayed on the door of the church, I did not know where else to go. A precarious structure of thick black wood, I always felt its prescence towering over me, patchouli smoke billowing from the thurible within in an attempt to drive the sickness from such a holy place. Father Enren drew back a small slit in the door and peered down, face sagging, as he saw the storm in my eyes and knew instantly what had happened.

"Lift up your shirt," he commanded, eyes roving for sign of the great blackened pustules that marked a plagued one.

Trembling, I obeyed, and he nodded curtly at my shame before pulling the great wooden door open. He stayed away from me still and ushered me to a pew as he hurried off to speak to someone else in hushed tones. I gazed up at the image of the Lord carved in marble set at the centre of the church, his expression pained, perhaps he understood my grief. I fell to my kneecaps on the stone floor and set my hands upon the ice cold purity of his pierced feet. "Lord," I whispered under my breath. "Oh Lord are you listening to me? Are you there? Can you please help me and save me, oh Lord?"

I gazed up at his contorted body and willed something to come, a feeling of peace, a message whispered over my shoulder, anything at all. But instead, I felt nothing, only the cool marble against my clammy hands. Then, a hard rap on my knuckles as Father Enren stared down at me with hellfire in his eyes, shaking his head. "Hands OFF the statue!" he barked.

I trembled before him again and wondered why the Lord, who touched lepers and sinners, would not want my hand upon his foot.

I do not know what they did with the bodies of my parents, but I slept fitfully in the church that night, sucking the iron-tang blood from my knuckles and dreaming of sweat-soaked sheets and bursting boils. I awoke with my face wet with tears as the lilac dawn licked the hillsides, and I was ushered back to my house. Most of our possessions were thrown upon the great bonfire that roared day and night in the centre of the village, and I watched as my bedclothes, a wooden doll my father carved, and my mother's dresses were smothered in thick smoke. The last memories of my family hardened into charcoal and the dust floated up into the heavens. Perhaps it is all now with the Lord.

I don't remember much from the year that followed, save for being lonely a lot. The population of the village had been decimated by the sickness, and as it slowly began to die out, no one had much interest in a girl alone wearing dirty clothes and begging for crusts of old bread. As time passed by, I found myself relishing in the quietude, and I learned to fend for myself. I pressed my little fingers into mud like treacle and clutched at earthy truffles. I roamed the woods a lot, searching for purple berries and ruddy mushrooms to nibble at. I shivered at night under a thin scrap of blanket I had stolen from the baker's washing line, and often there was a deep ache in my heart for my missing parents. Thankfully, we had one cow at the cottage and I knew how to milk her by myself, so as I sowed the seeds that my mother usually did and watched my tiny crops fail often for the first few years, I was grateful for her sweet milk to nourish my tired bones. No one cared or paid me any attention in those days, merely a lonely orphan girl living on the edge of the village. They saw me in church on Sundays, yes, but even then their dark looks and mutterings showed me I was dirty and unwanted. The plague passed as all things do, and the remaining rotting bodies were heaved onto a cart and taken somewhere out into the mist of the marshes. I tried not to think of the bodies sinking beneath the grey mire, their mouths full of mud.

As I grew older, I learned the ways of the seeds and the plants and began to know them as kin. When to plant them, how deep they should go, when to take them outside, whether to set them down in the shade or full sun. I tore up earthy root vegetables and roasted them on the open fireside, I squashed berries from the bushes into thick jams, and I began to know the meanings of the herbs my mother had grown. Chamomile, stinging nettle, feverfew, lemon balm, hyssop, poppy... I felt we knew one another and they were friends to me as no one else was. I wanted to heal and care for those who needed it, it felt like the only path for me now. I was good at it, and so folk slowly learned to come to me for aid.

Each day they came knocking at my door, and I found myself busy making salves and balms, creating bespoke tinctures, drying herbs and tending to my garden.

Often the days were so busy that I was late to church, and as I sat at the same pew my knuckles were bloodied at all those years ago, Father Enren eyes's still bored into me, despising. The hatred in his eyes confused me. He was a man of the cloth, he even carried a tiny Bible around his neck, the weight of the words bearing down his neck as a physical reminder of their importance. He stood before us and sang praises to the Lord and told us how we could be more like him. But wasn't the Lord kind to sinners? Didn't he help those in need, didn't he accept and love all for who they were? I could see none of this reflected in the man before me giving this sermon. His clammy hands grabbed my wrist as I turned to leave one Sunday, and he spoke in hushed tones as though it was of great shame to be seen with me. "Agatha, a word please."

I shook his hand from my arm and he brushed it over his robe as though to be rid of something foul. I felt much the same. "You are now of an age you should be married. It is... regrettable that you are so difficult to match, but I can find someone for you."

Did he expect me to fall at his feet with raindrops in my doe eyes, exclaiming of his generosity and kindness of spirit? No. I spoke now with no softness in my tone. "And what will a man have to offer me?"

He spluttered and choked out a laugh. "Why... all women must be married, of course! A man will protect you, he will tend to your land, he will build a home for you, he will give you purpose!"

Now it was my turn to laugh, but there was no tenderness there. "Father, all of these things I can do for myself. What good would a man do for me?"

I saw rage rising up through him, trembling through his yellowed eyeballs. The weakness of men, so quick to anger, so unable to contain their emotions. I couldn't help it that a smile flickered upon my lips. The hellfire of his anger flared behind those eyes.

"Agatha. You will be married, you will become a wife, you will bear children and you will do as you are bid. That is the place of a woman," he spat.

I reached into the pouch at my waist and drew out the dagger I used for maintaining the garden. Terror flickered in his expression, but I simply tore it through my raven-black hair and cropped it no longer than the men of the village. His sagging mouth drooped even further, aghast, as I cast the lengths of my hair to the church floor. "Then I shall no longer be a woman," I spat, and ran from the church, the dark door banging shut on me for the last time.

I did not grow my hair long and I did not wear a dress again. I retreated further into myself and dared not leave my cottage, lest he take me away. Each time I heard a knock upon my door I stiffened now, waiting for Father Enren and whichever man he deigned I marry. I buried myself in my work, the only thing I could think to do, and when my garden was full, I took to gathering herbs in the forest. One day as I walked, I heard a voice of honey and springtime coming from between the trees.

. . .

Bluebell, daffodil, where are thee?

Thy petals soft and thy fragrance sweet,

Dandelion, daisy, where are thee?

I wish to join you in the breeze, so free...

I crouched beneath the bracken, hair wild, and peered through the thorns, could this be a fae from ancient lore? A gentle spirit of the forest with a voice no sweet?

No, this was a woman.

Ember-orange hair tumbled past her waist, framing milk-white skin and emerald eyes. She wore a linen dress of the same deep green and it twirled about her figure as she danced through the trees, singing her song. My heartbeat began to quicken and I felt myself oddly breathless as I watched her, ethereal among the leaves. Mesmerised, I shifted my weight, and a twig cracked beneath me. She gasped and her head jolted to where I crouched, so I brushed the earth from my trousers and stood up hastily.

"I'm sorry, miss, I did not mean to frighten you. I was gathering mushrooms, you see." I gestured at the basket on my back. Suddenly I felt conscious of my wildness, my weirdness. So harsh and untamed against her delicate form.

Her fear turned to laughter and she simply smiled, as the way the crescent moon on autumn nights often melted my heart. "Oh no, I am no longer fearful. I know you... you are the healer, are you not?" She spoke softly and looked at me quizzically, eyes roving.

"Yes, my name is Agatha. What can I call you?"

"My name is Lily," she almost sang. My heart thrummed as she walked nearer to me and held out a dainty hand for me to shake. My soil-caked fingers reached out but I pulled away quickly at the thought I might dirty her. She saw my reaction and laughed again like the pealing of bells as she pulled it back to hers, grasping it firmly. "Everything comes from the earth, does it not? What do I have to be wary of some mud?"

She crouched down, two fingers gliding through the thick earth, and I watched in shock as she ran them over her cheeks. Battle-paint of the forest indeed. I laughed, and let her gentle fingers smear the marks on my skin too as my breath caught in my throat. I knew her then to be as strong and fearless as an ox inside. We chatted lightly for a while of small things, and I was reluctant to let her go, but she curtsied and returned to her song, skipping away between the trees as she did so.

Father Enren made his distaste of me and my work clear, and he did not refrain from saying so. I heard that he often spoke ill of me to others, spreading strange rumours about the wild thing I had become that roamed among them, neither man nor woman. The church marked a black abyss on the landscape to me now, and I felt unwelcome and fearful before the sight of our marble Lord. Walking through the village made me weary and I tried to avoid it as much as I could, I was bored of their constant whisperings and babbling. I wanted to simply do my work, but even now my cottage began to feel claustrophobic and unsafe.

I took to wandering the marshlands outside of the village where I found plants I had not seen before and felt peace I could not attain at my cottage. Grey grasses, curled leaves and peculiar bog flowers so radiant in their ugliness. Without thinking, I found that I began to gather wood and carry it with me each day, slowly building a new home for myself piece by piece. On the night a full moon smiled upon the bog water, it was complete. A veritable shack of a cabin set upon the firm places of the marsh, and oh how I loved it. There I sat night after night with my feet warming by the fire, a pot of tea on to boil and a place set out for two. For yes I was alone, for all but my Lily.

And she came to me often.

When the land was sun-soaked and the sky so golden it felt like honey smothered us in its sweet song, Lily and I would wander the forest together, gazing at flowers and whispering strange nothings to the insects that dwelled under the rocks. She was always so alight and alive, bursting with storm-fuelled passion, and it brought out the same in me. Often we walked, hand in hand among the trees. We lay upon the daisy grass and spoke in our made-up language, giggling at nothing and making shapes of the clouds. And when the land was misted and storm-thick, she would come to my bog house and we would wiggle our toes together by the peat fire, sharing spiced rock cakes and rose petal tea.

Oh my Lily, my dearest Lily.

Some of the village folk still visited me in those days, despite Father Enren's warning. The heart can become desperate so quickly, and I had answers no other could give. When the bog-stench was thick and the weary sunlight broke through the mist, they still came to me. Blackened fingernails and mud-caked eyelashes, often I wandered into the smell of the gaping marsh. They feared me, now, I knew it. They whispered of me and my strange ways. The way I took to roaming the fen alone for hours at a time, the way the vultures flocked to me as I sat under the shade of the reeds, so peculiar I was. All alone with wise knowings of the land and the plants beneath my feet.

Yet still, they still sought me out, rapping bloody knuckles on my door and begging me for elixirs and medicine. They needed me. "Agatha", they whined. "My wife is late to begin her labours, what can you give her?"

"Agatha, please help me with the festering wound on my leg," they whimpered.

Tar-black wounds, womb wisdom, rotten teeth. I helped them all. Not one did I turn away. I sat with mothers labouring for fifty hours, I sewed up injuries, I fed children medicine by the ladle as I had my own parents.

They needed me, until they didn't.

The village grew as the years passed, huts became stone structures and herbs became medicine passed between the hands of righteous men. It was unnatural, they began to say, for someone to live alone such as me. Not right, they said, for me to be so learned of the bog and its ways. Evil, they began to whisper, that I stalk the marsh at night. Healing and wise soon became strange and unwelcome.

The rapping on my door came less, and I found myself at a loss of what to fill my days with now that I could no longer heal. I spoke to the Lord a few times over the years and asked where he had gone, if he really felt the way Father Enren told me he did. But as I whispered my strange prayers into the mud, I felt nothing. Things darken often with no warning, this was a harsh truth I learnt as a child. Father Enren soon began to tell them I was evil, taken over by the devil, and I would not take a husband and do as I was told. It mattered not to me, I did not need their trust and friendship, but when my Lily came rapping upon my door with those soft white hands, and she buried herself in me in floods of tears, panic flickered within me. I rested her gentle face upon my heart and cradled her as she wept, laying soft kisses upon her hair of flame.

"What is it, Lily, my love?" I whispered into her flesh.

Her body wracked with sobs, those emerald eyes peered into my own and I felt my heart crack like my mother's had so many years ago. "I am to be married, my dear Agatha, I am to be sent to the house of the blacksmith and made to be his wife. I shall have to bear his children, care for him, and lie in bed with him at night." She whined and buried herself deeper into the folds of my blanket.

I knew then that I would not be permitted to see Lily again. Who would let their wife wander off to see the strange evil creature that lived in the bog? No, I would not see her again. I whispered comforts that meant nothing as I pressed her to me and buried a farewell deep into my heart. We should have known that it would not last, we would never be free to be together. I held that porcelain face in my hands, so dainty looking to an outsider, but one I knew as so wild, so free, so fearless. She had never distrusted me, she had never been afraid, she had always come to me and loved me for who I was. Betwixt and between. To see fear brimming those eyes was a hurt I could not endure. I pressed my lips to hers and tasted sweet honey cakes and rose petals. My Lily, my love, no longer mine.

She stayed with me that night and we wound around one another, holding each other tight as though that would stop her from having to leave in the morning. I kissed her with a heartsick longing and let her go for the final time. A pastel dawn crept in through the edges of the window, so beautiful it was almost mocking, and as the crow called good morning I wished him be struck down so as to let our lover's night linger.

Her skin was paler than usual, and she would not eat the treacle loaf I had set out to warm on the hearth, only sip at the chamomile tea and gaze into nothingness with empty eyes. I kissed her forehead and bade her farewell, and she left me then, wordlessly. Now she was gone, an emptiness lingered and a tear fell down my cheek. I exhaled deeply and let them fall, now I had nothing left.

In the years that followed I withdrew entirely, choosing to speak only to the plants, often taking to pressing my limbs into the quagmire and letting the stench cover me. Sweet water of the bog, you know me well. What prayers I had for the Lord now spilled from my cracked lips into the rotten earth, and I felt it answer me and hold me each day that went by. The infrequent rapping at my door now ceased entirely, though I would not have answered it anyway. The villagers seethed with hatred for me, I knew it. Father Enren grew old, but his obsession with me festered into something putrid.

And so, they came for me. I was not surprised, I had been expecting this for many years. They came for me with torches and rope, braying on my door and smashing at my bog house until the wood collapsed and fell into the mire. Down tumbled my home, sweet cakes and soft blankets crushed under the moss-coated roof. I did not struggle as they pulled me from my home, I simply waved farewell to my garden. The last farewell I would make. And so they bound my arms and bound my legs, and to each they tied slabs of white marble stone. "Witch, witch, witch," they chanted, as they heaved me up high and held me above their heads.

I did not feel fear, instead I felt nothing. They swung my aching body and cast me into the festering marshland. The last thing I saw above this ground were manic faces, lit by flickering firelight, jeering as my body sank deeper into the grey sludge. The rot coated my eyeballs, filled my gaping mouth and tumbled down my throat as the air left my body.

But in the darkness of the bog, it remembered me. For the land knows, and the land remembers.

Did you know that bodies do not decompose in a bog? No, the skin blackens and turns hard like leather. The bones remain, brittle and preserved, and even the hair stays stuck upon the scalp. And so I remained also, and became part of the gentle marshland I loved so much. I had given myself to it in life, and so in death the spirit of the bog flowed within me and I became part of it. Time did not exist, seconds and eons passed in my place of peace and quietude, free to be myself. Nature knows that her creatures come in many forms, all connected through one spirit. Many bodies I found in its depths, the plague bodies, lost travellers, and eventually, my parents. I stretched out my mud fingers and a bog flower bloomed above them as I wished them a deep rest. And there I remained, part of the land as the guardian of the bog.

One morning in early spring, I felt a strange sensation upon the quagmire, like a gentle kiss planted upon the mud. As I roamed the land within myself, I noticed something so out of place - a single white lily blooming upon the bog. I reached my vine-fingers out and found her there, my Lily, cast herself into the bog. Red hair of sunset skies, unrotted forever. I pressed her to my spirit as breath left her and felt her smile and kiss upon me with tears of joy.

"Oh Agatha, I came for you. I knew you would be here."

"Yes, my love, I am here. And so are you. And we always will be."

And so our spirits joined the misted marsh, and we danced together beneath the mud, into the infinite expanse of the void forever.

4

FERAL

She appeared to me first with knees scuffed raw from crawling through the bracken's unforgiving teeth. What a strange sight, for one of her kind. Dress torn, hair wild, eyes even wilder, she did not seem to notice the drip of hot blood down her tiny legs. How peculiar she was. Her cheeks were rose-touched with youth's generous swell, flushed with the joy of childhood in summer. For all human things must come to an end, and the joy of that makes those days taste extra sweet. Their years are unfamiliar to me, and therefore, I cannot say with certainty how old she was, but she was small, even for a human. A mass of dark curls fell about her plump cheeks, bark-brown eyes wide and brimming with a curiosity I had forgotten existed.

In those days, there weren't many of us left. Some had chosen to pass from this world, and the few of us that remained led a quiet existence in the recesses of the earth, away from the burden of civilization. In the early days of creation, it was not so bad as when this little one came to me.

I was there, you see.

I was there when the first sunrise yawned and stretched himself out in the endless skies, watching as he kissed the earth and collapsed beyond the horizon. I was there when ice scarred and melted into the vast seas, when strange creatures stalked the deserts and human folk did not yet wander. In those days, tree spirits lazed by summer pools of cerulean, and the woodland queen sang often. How quiet it was now, yet how loud it had become.

I watched the world throughout the long days of my life, and I was there when the first human blinked their sticky eyes into existence. In the early days of the earth, we existed together, sharing the great caverns and woodlands of the West, but as the villages unfolded, and their kind grew in number, I knew it was safer for me to begin my retreat. And so, I spread my wings and took off into the place where the clouds thickened above the river and gazed down at their tiny dwellings for the last time. As the smoke billowed from chimneys, I bade a small farewell and nestled it deep within my immortal heart. And so I went into the mountains, to rest and dream in a slumber as deep as the ocean realms.

I ventured far into the dark chasms and there I found other creatures hiding also. I did not ask their names, knowing the power of naming things, but passed them silently and they observed me as they chattered among themselves, starlight whispers still clinging on to forgotten magics. Here it was cool and black, and I set my ice-blooded body down and rested awhile. For many moon cycles I slumbered, dreaming of soft things under her milky light, fae eyes staring out at me from cave walls and reflecting in my scales all the while. The rats found me after a time, tiny paws scuffling, curious and afraid. I admit I have a distaste for rats, the way they look at me in fear and disgust, the way they nibble at one another and tell tales of me that are not true.

But I did not see a human for aeons, until the day she came. Yes, for she came, and she was not afraid of me.

There she stood, wild-eyed and feral-faced, wandering the winding tunnels of this blackened place. The joy of curiosity swiftly darkened, and tears brimmed her eyes as she spiralled into the realisation that she was lost. She let out a silent sob that shook the very marrow of me and sat on the floor by my side, though I and the stone had a likeness, and she did notice me yet. I don't like to admit it, but I was frightened. I had not seen the likes of her for an age, and I did not know what to do. But as I saw her tear drops fall fat and timid, pity soaked me, and I unlinked myself from the vast stone walls. I moved gently, raising my head tentatively at first, so that she could see she was not alone. She turned to me, quivering, but immediately, her tears stopped. Rat-prejudiced, I had thought she would run, but she did not. Her river eyes filled with wonder, and I felt a courage stirring from deep inside her, she was not afraid of me. I reached out cautiously with my knowing and brushed up against her young mind, yet she did not recoil. I spoke to her then in an ancient language that has no words and revealed the way she must leave through the winding passageways. She reached a hand to me, but I pulled away, afraid, and she ran from the cave laughing gleefully.

After she had left, I thought myself foolish, and wondered if I should have revealed my location to one of them, and one so young at that. I fretted and paced in a way I had not done since I roamed freely, and regretted becoming entangled with their world once more. I hoped she would not come back to visit me, and I hoped she would keep me a secret. Perhaps if she spoke of me now, no one would pay her any mind. I settled eventually and curled up against the damp stone, journeying to my familiar dreams again. But three moon cycles later, she came to seek me out. She did not try to touch me again, but she sat and chittered to me in the strangest way. Her young speech was often babbling and shrill, but somehow, I did not mind. I sat silently, unmoving, as she told me of her life in the village on the mountainside, of her mother who baked honey cakes and her father who built houses. She told me of many things I had almost forgotten, of how fat berries tasted when ripe in late summer, of her orange tabby cat and his poor hunting skills, and of her favourite storybook filled with castles and warriors. But I was too afraid to reply.

When she left, I felt strangely morose, and wished I had said something. Perhaps she thought me dumb and would now not return to tell me more stories of honey cakes and tabby cats. The peace I had built over aeons had slipped, and I felt regret burrow into the recesses of my bones. But to my unexpected joy, she did return, and with her brought tales of sunshine dappled through oak leaves and raindrops falling on bare skin. She talked for hours and brought me things to look at, not knowing I had seen everything there was to see. She came often in those early days, and she asked me to leave the cave and play with her in the woods, but still, I stayed silent. I knew I had disappointed her, but I thought on what she said, and as the days passed by, I wondered often how much had changed since I had begun my slumber in the mountains.

On a fine morning in midsummer, I summoned a butterfly's wing of courage from a place deep in my heart, shook the moss from my heavy body and ventured from the cave. The first golden drop of sunlight on my skin was nourishing and sweet, and I scented the wildflowers as they swayed on the hillside. I walked gently and quietly, ready to flee at a moment's notice, but no danger came. Testing further, I stretched my wings and rested awhile down by the river, drinking crystal from its depths and exhaling the cobwebs from my ancient bones.

She came to me again, or rather, I came to her. I heard her laughter first, like the tumble of a stream, and I saw her playing in the woods. To an outsider, she may have looked alone, but my eyes watched as she conversed with the in-between creatures that human folk could rarely see. She sang with them songs built with strange melodies, endured their endless tricksy riddles, and in her hands, twigs became magic wands, leaves became crowns. She saw me creeping and gasped, eyes alight. The fae fled at my arrival, they still feared me. But she did not.

Instead, she reached into her pocket and took from it a swollen pink berry, extending her hand to me. Slowly, carefully, I took it from her fingers and let the sweetness explode in my mouth. Tart and fresh like warm days that feel unending. She set her hand upon my scales, and I did not shy away from her this time. At her touch, I felt our minds join and she knew me as I knew her. She ran her fingers down my shimmering body, and I felt the question in my mind. I bowed my head as she pulled herself up, sitting astride me, and I felt the joy soar through her heart. I had not flown for thousands of years, but it was no hardship to me. Like a breath of fresh air, I tore upwards and inhaled the sky. She whooped and shrieked, and her thrill flowed into my wings. She sang to me as we flew together, human songs of warriors and kings, and I sang to her in my own way, and told her of hidden places, secret paths, and ancient beings older than time itself. After I time, I shared my name with her, *Aina*, which means 'always and forever'.

It seemed I only blinked, and she had grown taller, yet she still came to me often, and we were like one in those days. She showed me the small joys of human life, and I showed her the deep tranquillity of mine, and together we rode through the night sky, sharing memories and dreams. The moon sighed overhead, as if remembering an old memory, and I looked forward to our meetings as she brought me honey cakes and sweet berries. But their lives are so short, and these years blur so quickly for me. One day, tall and strong, she came to me with a swell in her belly and a glow on her skin. I scented the infant inside of her and felt it growing, filled with vigour. She saw me less frequently in those years, but time means little to me, falling like acorns in autumn, and I did not worry. We rode together and she whispered to me of the babe, who had grown strong and lithe. She told me she had named it after me, Aina, and I felt my stone heart would shatter from joy.

I blinked again and she came to me with hair flossed and white like winter's first frost. Deep oak-bark lines were etched on her face, and she could no longer summon the strength to ride me. Instead, she sat softly among the dead leaves, tucked into the coil of my tail as she had as a child, and told me tales of her life and her daughter. The last time I saw her, she walked slowly into the cave with a stick to support her and kissed me gently on the head. We sat in the quietude and enjoyed one another's silent company.

She did not come again.

A little time after, I felt her spirit pass into the realm of others where myself and the fair folk dwell. I placed her farewell into my heart where it joined so many others I had given over the years and tucked it in safely. I did not miss her, for she was with me always.

The years that followed passed gently, and I thought of my dear friend often, remembering to venture out and taste the air of each season as she had so encouraged me. I lapped honeysuckle and watched the first shoots of spring as though I saw them for the first time through her sparkling childlike eyes. When the summer berries drooped fat and heavy on the bushes, I thought of her. Many seasons passed by, and I dreamed in quietude, nestled into the rock, until one day a scuffling of the floor awoke me. Heavy-lidded, I moved cautiously and scanned the cave for the visitor. Rats? No. I scented the air and my eyes focused. No, I knew this one.

Before me stood a woman, tall and strong with wild dark hair and round riverbed eyes. Though her hands trembled and brimmed with tears, she smiled and began to laugh, shaking her head. A letter was clutched in her quaking hands. I greeted her in my own way and sent a shiver of reassurance through her bones. I felt her hang on to it with every fibre of her being and she approached, cautious fingers outstretched. I moved towards her and she set a hand upon my scales, sending sparks through our bodies.

Yes, I knew this one.

Aina.

Adder's Song

The moor-wind tastes of heather and mist,

dusty lilac buds form in the folds of my tongue,

gorse-prickled goosebumps soft as butterfly wings.

Crouching in the bracken clothed in thorn-torn rags,

knocking knees black with blood-crust and bramble.

Grey peat squelches between gnarled toes,

a hare's-lair, a secret place, bog-moss and worms.

Snake-scales bending spines in the woven grass.

OCEAN VAST OF BRINE AND BONE
WHISPERED WATERS CALL ME HOME

Hare-Hearted

I have tried to be dainty.

Soft-footed, hare-hearted, dress trailing through meadow-daisies,

Honeyed poetry and doe eyes filled with gently spoken promises,

But something rough gets caught in my throat.

A raw cough, a cacophony of confrontational cussing,

Rock-grit is mashed in the tread of my heavy boot-falls.

Unwashed, unkempt, blackened fingernails half-chewed again,

Heavy hands slam, cramming, jamming, goddamn -

I don't even know how to *breathe* as gently as her.

A little rough around the edges instead, that's how I'll be.

5
WAVES

It had been thirty days since his ship had left the shore. It was normal, they said, for a woman to be left alone like this. I was to do my duty, they said, and care for our home while he was away. I'd first locked eyes with him when I was in my teen years, pink-cheeked with eyelashes coated in naivety. The village market was better in those days, and all the fish was fresh from our shores. I knew he would be there each Sunday, slinging his great net and hauling crab from his boat. And so I went, each week, and bought their soft bodies from him.

He was older than me, though still young, with sun-tanned arms roped in muscle. I remember the way his hair fell into his eyes. those eyes so vast and blue. Deep blue like the ocean he loved so much. Those sea-spray eyes sparkled with mischief, a lust for adventure. Even then I knew I would never be able to keep him happy. Even then I knew I would never be enough. Me and the sea, how could I compare to her rolling curves? The way she whispered on the shoreline and tickled a man's skin with salt spray. The way she called to them with her caress on the pale sand.

But I fell in love with him anyway.

The first time I felt true joy was when we crossed the threshold into our cottage. White bricked and crusted in sea salt, ocean grass swaying in the tiny garden. We laughed a lot and held each other's faces, shared sardines on the patio during long summer days, and tasted the season's first strawberries with lashings of cream. We were young lovers giddy with new things and the promise of tomorrow, it felt like it would never end. He took me often on his boat and I watched him haul the net. It often rained and we were drenched in salt water and sky tears, but I did not care. He told me that he loved me often, and I believed the words he spoke, in a way. I believed that he wanted to love me. And I resolved to try and make him.

I brought the sea into our home for him, thinking it would be enough. I painted our home pale blue and hung up water-colour paintings of starfish and lighthouses. I dotted seashells on the surfaces and even the bedsheets were a deep indigo, like being folded into the waves. I let him go on his boat and leave me each day, I could do nothing but watch him leave in the distance and wait for his return. I tore the crab claws apart and cooked them well, and we dined often on salt flesh and shared kisses over salmon.

But still, in those days of lovesickness, I caught him staring at her.

Yes, her.

Often, I would find him, elbows on the windowsill, staring out at her deep waters, pining for her cool embrace. His eyes misted over with seasick longing, and I knew he wished to taste her salt. I pulled him back to my warm arms time and time again, but a layer of brine began to form between us. My children never lived past a week old, and as I watched their tiny bodies offer up a last breath, all I could think of was how cursed I was. How she had cursed me.

He buried our children in the garden with no gravestone, and I set a conch on the mounds. I wondered if he thought they human enough to warrant a gravestone, but I did not ask. He mourned with me, but I knew he was angry, I was failing him. I watched summer days pass and other little boys grow older, splashing on the shoreline, the ocean hypnotising them already. I knew he watched them too, how she tickled their feet, how they lay back on her soothing presence and felt peace.

We spoke less, and he started leaving me more and more, clambering into the folds of wet wood and heading out into the ocean with his fishing nets, promising fat fish and salty crab on his return. I knew the life of a fisherman, and it seemed to me that his days offshore stretched longer and longer. I noticed his brow begin to furrow and the lines of age etching into his skin, the sparkle in those blue eyes began to dim when he was with me, I could not deny it, and so to the boat he returned.

And now he had gone. Thirty days had passed, and many of my nights had been fitful and sleepless. As I lay there between my sea-blue covers, all I could hear was her mocking me, pushing herself closer and closer towards our home as the tide came in. She thrummed against my senses, laughing at me. But I knew she rocked him gently out on her open waters, lulling him side to side into a deep, dreamless sleep. I seethed with anger and banged the window shut, but it was not enough to soothe her incessant scratching in the recesses of my brain.

Several market days had passed, and I had not visited the village. I felt I had become ill, and I had no desire to be seen by others, to purchase fish that came from her waters. Instead, I chose to remain in the cottage, going hungry rather than go to the market where the watchful eyes of others followed me, shaking their heads and sighing softly when they saw me. They pitied me. Me, a mother to no one except myself. Me, a woman so foul a man would rather get lost at sea than sleep next to. Those days began to blend into one, and I did not carry out my wifely duties. Washing day came and went, and clothes were piled high, dirty in the corners of the cottage.

One fitful night I awoke in a cold sweat and tore the bedding from my skin. I could feel the salt crusting on my flesh, and I could not bear to be with her a moment longer. I tore the ocean blankets from the bed and ran into the garden, standing before the graves of my children. The moon was full and heavy that night, and I felt she smiled upon me and approved of my doings. I piled driftwood high and set it alight, until a great roaring flame danced before me. I cast the bedding into the fire and cackled with glee as I watched the flames envelop it and take her down. But as the flames died in the early hours of the morning and the moon madness of the previous night left me, I saw her again in the distance, pulling and pushing, in and out, undefeated. I had not killed her.

Bed bugs, I told the neighbours. Such a shame, they were our favourite sheets. There was nothing for it but to burn them. They exchanged glances and smiled at me sadly, they did not believe there was anything that was 'ours' anymore. Thirty days soon became sixty, and I had eaten only little, hard crusts of bread and butter without salt. I paced the cottage and ran my hands through my thinning hair, watching from the window for the bob of his white and red boat.

The gulls game to me, scuffling around the grave mounds and begging for scraps of bread. I found myself cawing with them sometimes. I reached my hands to touch one, but they evaded me. I began to scratch at the wall with the pointed edge of seashells, etching strange curses no one would ever read. I cannot remember if I ever slept through a full night in those days, only that dreams of eels plagued me, and I felt their noose bodies around my neck as I awoke in cold sweats. I often looked to the fisher rope in the cupboard and wondered if it would feel eel-like around my neck too.

I put it away.

On the ninetieth day, I was hairless. I had not seen my neighbours for over a month, and I wondered if they thought I had died or fled. Would anyone come for me? Would anyone come and check on me? I sat by the window as I did every day, my eyes glazed over as I stared out at the beach. I watched the waters nudge a great mound to the shoreline. Driftwood? A large fish or even a dolphin? I had sworn I would stay away from her, but I'll admit, my curiosity got the better of me. My body trembled and I felt strength fade from my muscles, but I tore my rotting bones from the cottage and ventured down to the beach. My toes sank into the grey sand as I moved towards the shoreline, and that's when I saw him.

Sea-bloated with white flesh falling away from bone, my husband lay there on the sand, murdered by his mistress. I looked into those blue eyes, now glassy and lifeless, and I felt rage. Confusion. She had stolen him and disposed of him.

I couldn't take it anymore; I would show her how I felt. I ran down to the shoreline and pounded at the water in my rage, her salty pools stinging my eyes as she splashed back at me. She was a good fighter. I let out a wail and found it was a seagull's cry, choking my throat. I walked into the waves in my dress and felt it pool around me as it filled with icy water. She enveloped my skin, and my salty tears tumbled into her salt water as my feet tore on the coral beneath me. I shrieked in confusion, begging her to tell me why and offer a semblance of explanation. I submerged my head under her depths, and as I let the water fill my lungs, I heard an eel's whisper in my ear.

Sister, the sea is not your enemy.

I have no reason, for this is my nature.

6
ICE

For as long as I can remember, I have dreamed of ice.

Not November's hesitant snowfall or the dusting of winter's first kiss, tumbling from the heavens as dandelion seed on a breeze. Not rolling moorland of ivory bliss and sunlight dappling through dancing flakes.

No, I dreamed of ice.

Of black ice, of blue ice. Knife-edge shards of crystal glass dipped in the poison of a bitter January winter. I dreamed of the polar bear's secrets and snowstorms, of lightning and molten steel.

I watched my brothers and sisters as lithe children of spring, budding in the haze of morning light and drinking sweet dew from crocus petals. There they were, all rose-cheeked with plump little hands clutching at strawberries and cream. I watched as they pressed rosemary seeds into the crumbling earth and willed the sun to drag them upwards. He listened. Their laughter was like a tumbling brook, giggling among one another as they twirled in the bluebell wood.

But I? I was a child of winter, and I had always dreamed of ice.

I had come early, mother told me. My five siblings flourished in March and April, and I had been a hard labour, wrought with trouble and pain for her. I had come when January kissed February, on the bitter night of a snowstorm. I had almost not made it into this world, she told me, she had collapsed in the barn and a snowdrift covered the doorway. There she writhed in torment on the bloodied hay as the cows cried out along with her and the storm summoned me into this world. My family were tall and broad, with glowing skin and a full head of dark hair, impossibly beautiful and filled with oxen strength. But I was born sickly and small, my skin lacked substance and my pale hair was fine and breakable. I cried often as a child, and I did not care for my mother's milk. My siblings were too afraid to play with me, so breakable and strange, and my father only looked at me with anger in his eyes. How could I be his child, so different from the others? But my mother loved me. I believe only I noticed it, but she held me closer than the other children, she left kisses on my forehead more often, and she sang strange lullabies to me.

I grew slowly, but I did grow. I always was weak, and though they gave me lighter jobs, I was still never any good. My father struck me often for a dropped pail of milk, wasted cream running through the cracks in the barn floor. I deserved it. I could not help them push the bales of hay or harvest the crop, for my body was too tender and fragile. The sweltering sun-sickness of the summer days drew strength from my bones, and often I was taken ill, lying in bed for weeks at a time, my skin yellowing and my body becoming even thinner. My father cursed me when he thought I could not hear and called me lazy and ungrateful. My brother repeated his words and spoke of it to my siblings, and so, they began to hate me. They did not invite me to their games, their fear mingled with hatred, and I grew so lonesome.

The only bliss in my young years was when I closed my weary eyes and surrendered to sleep. I dreamt that great avalanches of thick snow would rush upon me and bury me until my lungs filled with ice and I could no longer breathe. The feel of glaciers against my sun-burned skin soothed my sickness and felt like a drink of water to me. Even in the throes of fever dreams, I always dreamed of ice.

And so, when he came for me, I went willingly.

Dusk had settled upon the land and a lilac haze stretched itself out across the fading sky. It was the first snowfall of the year, unnaturally cold too early. There was a gentle knock at the door, so soft, that to me it sounded more like snowflakes collapsing onto fresh snow. My family looked to each other, concerned, and my father stood to open the door. But I knew who it was without looking, and I ran before his angry eyes and tore it open. A ghostly wash of cold enveloped me and soothed my sickness, and then I set my eyes upon him.

My father staggered backwards in fear and reached behind the door to pick up the axe that rested against the wall there. He stood firm, though I detected a tremble in his voice, and demanded to know who the stranger was. My siblings ran to the door, cowering behind my father, but my mother stood in silence, unafraid, a single silver tear tumbling down her face. A creature stood in the doorway, snow gathering in a cloud around him. Tall, taller than my father, with skin and eyes as white as fallen snow. His silver hair fell long and straight down past his knees, and on the top of his head, two speckled antlers stretched upwards. He wore a crown of holly with berries in full winter ripeness and draped upon his body were furs of pure white. Although darkness had begun to blanket the land, a peculiar lunar light shone from his skin, and snowflakes seemed to fall from his fingertips. He spoke no words aloud, but simply stretched out his hand, and I took it willingly. I was not afraid.

My mother threw her head back and wailed in a way that only mothers can, the pain sharp as an icicle's edge, for she knew him by name. Her wolf howls faded into the night air as she dropped to her knees, begging me to stay, but my father remained expressionless. One less mouth to feed. My siblings did not say a word to me, but simply stood, mouths agape, and so I left them with no fond farewells. I knew I would never see any of them again.

And so, I took the deer-man's hand, and felt it cool in my grip. I wiped my mother's tears from her face and walked with him away from my home. No, not my home. I looked back only once, at the flickering window candlelight growing smaller in the distance, and saw that the stranger had left no footprints in the freshly fallen snow. No speech needed to pass between us, I followed him wordlessly. His chariot lay before the pine forest, and I couldn't stifle the gasp that spilled from my lips as I looked upon it. A thousand antlers joined together to form its peculiar shape, sleigh bottomed against the snow, winding around one another to create a seat draped in furs. At the front, a polar bear with white eyes scuffled and stared at me, bemused. The brown bears of our woods had always instilled fear within me, and my father had often returned from a hunt early rather than face them. And yet, this strange white bear did not scare me. I took the deer-man's hand and climbed upon the sleigh, finding comfort on his deer-wrought vessel. Nestled in the thick furs of animals I did not recognise, I slumbered awhile, returning to my familiar dream.

But when I awoke, I saw my dream with waking eyes. White mountains cloaked in snow jewels stood tall against the horizon, beckoning. I descended the chariot and walked by his side, our footfalls silent on the soft snow. He did not look at me. He did not need to. The air tasted sweet like crushed peppermint and snowdrops, and I drank in the glorious fragrance of my dreams. Oh, how long I had waited to bask here in the snowfall. We walked until we reached a castle carved of pure ice. In my dreams I saw ice of black and blue and had thought it to be a terrible evil I needed purged from me, but now it made sense. Blue it sparkled in the gentle white light, great pillars extending upwards carved into intricate patterns, impossibly ornate. We moved through the great keep, still our footfalls silent on the ice-floor, and entered the throne room. Snow-dusted icicles burst up from the ground as though a living creature, forming the mighty throne that sat there.

I knew what must happen. And so, I felt my life fall away. I gave it up easily, like exhaling or closing my eyes. Visions fluttered through my mind on silver butterfly wings, the strike of my father's hand against my cheek, the bruises from other children, the tricks they played upon me. And the worst pain of all, the pain of unbelonging. I collapsed upon the icicle throne and heaved, releasing my life, and stepping into a new one. How long I lay there, I cannot say, perhaps a second, perhaps one thousand years, it's all the same. When I awoke, the deer-man knelt before me, his pale eyes brimming with sorrow and joy. He grasped an antler with each gloved hand and tore them from his head, his wolf howls dancing through the ice glass of the castle. He presented them to me, head bloody and bowed, and I took them from him. I set my fingers under his chin and willed his eyes to look up towards me. I leant down to set a snowflake's kiss upon his forehead. "Thank you, father," I whispered, like a cold winter breeze.

A smile stretched across his face and fell like frost on the wind, his body shattered into uncountable snowflakes and faded into the ether.

I stood awhile in the air where he had knelt, breathing in his scent of woodsmoke and pine, of snowstorms and deer skin, and then I took his antlers outside. The chariot awaited me there, and with a touch, his antlers melded into the others, joining our forefathers and foremothers in the eternal journey. I rested a hand of friendship upon the cheek of the white bear and climbed into the sleigh. I felt the pieces settling into my heart; peace, contentment, belonging, and even as I sat, I felt strength flow through my bones. Atop my head, bones were forming, and antlers sprung from my flesh. I set my hands upon the reins; I had a job to do. A purpose. The bear leapt and we ran through the night sky, blanketing the realms in winter's sweet kiss.

7

BIRD-BONED

Hush... can you hear it? The fluttering of wings, the tip-tap of hardened claw. Quieter, let your footsteps fall gently. Can you hear the croak deep from hollow throat, the soft caw on the spring breeze? There she roams, bird-boned, feather-flocked, moving this way, that way, through the forest of pines. Sweet child of wild blueberries and mountain thyme, lost and yet not lost. Missing and yet found. Incomplete and yet whole.

Anika, we called her in human tongue, and I knew I would love her from the moment I set my eyes upon her, delicate as she was. A wandering scribe, I had roamed the heather-peppered hills and twisted footpaths for most of my life with naught but a weathered pack upon my back, a set of ink and quills, and folds of thick parchment to work my trade. A man destined to roam, never to settle, I needed nothing more than the wind through my hair and the sound of the brook as I slept beneath the stars by a dwindling fireside. I was quite content to travel through villages and bustling towns, stopping for a short while to taste the local ales and replenish my supplies, but never one to stay in one place for too long.

Until I saw Anika.

Spring had just started to tickle the hillsides, butter-yellow flower petals sprung up from the earth and sunlight filtered through soft rainfall, nourishing the land. I found myself in a small village on the edge of the great evergreen forest, Pine-hollow, they called it. I needed a fresh load of bread and some dried meats, new inks and perhaps even a lighter cloak for the warmer days to come, if I had the coin. I did not kid myself that the folk of this village would need a scriber's hand, most of them could not read and had no need for learning it either. No, this would simply be a rest stop. As I wandered the narrow streets and rapped on the doors of merchants selling leatherworks, herbal tinctures and swathes of rough fabrics, I began to wonder if I would be able to find ink at all, perhaps they simply had no purpose for it.

I passed through the Sunday market and followed my nose to the baker's wares, deciding on a dark, sweet loaf that would keep well on my travels. I sipped at the hoppy ale from the local brewer and pondered awhile as I perched myself on a wooden bench, perhaps tomorrow I would leave and find somewhere else to stay. I watched a dark bird fly far up over-head and absent-mindedly followed his route through the sky, so free and wild. My eye travelled with him until he ducked behind the trees out of my sight, and that was when my eyes pulled me to her.

There she stood behind her market stall, smiling softly up at the trees, her eyes alight with the joy of the same bird that had caught my eye. A slender woman, with tar-black hair bound into braids and wide eyes as grey as winter's sky, I spotted the earthenware pots upon her table and felt myself pulled towards them. Or her. She looked up and cocked her head at me, a stranger to these parts. I touched my hand to hat in friendly greeting and smiled at her with as much warmth as I could muster before speaking gently. “My lady, could you tell me what you carry in these pots?” I enquired.

She met my gaze and tucked her stray hairs behind her ears as she spoke. “Indeed, I am a seller of dyes.” She lifted one of the lids and inside lay a thick powder of emerald green, ready to be mixed with water and used for dye. “Do you need something, sir?”

“I am a scribe, you see, and I’m looking for inks so that I can write.” I pulled out my old pots from within my cloak and showed her the dried remnants that needed replacing.

She considered for a moment before replying. “I can make you inks of indigo, of black, and of scarlet. But it will take me one week, will you still be here, traveller?”

I paused, usually I would not wish to remain somewhere so long, but something of this woman stopped me in my tracks. “I will be, my lady.”

She chuckled. “Please, I am no lady, my name is Anika. And what can I call you, sir?”

“I am Terren.” I smiled.

“Terren. Please come to my house in one week, I live in the wooden cabin on the edge of the pine forest. I will have your inks.”

I set my coin purse into her hands as a goodwill gesture that I would not leave, and tipped my hat once more as I made my way back to the inn with a warmth in my heart.

All week as I wandered the same streets of the tiny village again and again, I thought of Anika and her inks. I hadn't even stopped to wonder of their quality and her skill, and I hoped it would be good enough for the work I wished to undertake. I prided myself on my handiwork, not just words, but illustrations of exotic animals, peculiar plants and castles where high lords and princesses gazed out from the tower windows. Though I often found myself writing letters and notices, books were my love, and I had spent many an hour copying the pages of ancient tomes. I even found myself so bold as to ask some of the villagers about Anika, and was surprised by their response. Often she could be seen dancing on the pine needles as if they caused her no pain, they said. She was found shaking them from her skirts and laughing in a strange cawing fashion with the wild birds. She spent her time alone in the pine forest, gathering berries and plants for dye. They shook their heads at her, so fanciful, so ungrounded.

On the following Sunday I followed the track up to the edge of the evergreen woods and saw the little wooden cabin in the distance. Such a peculiar building, it appeared to be crafted from bundles of large sticks bound together rather than the neat wooden logs I was accustomed to seeing. Smoke billowed up from out of the chimney, welcoming this stranger. I saw her coal-black hair flowing in the garden and I watched her as I made my way to her house. Strange and beautiful Anika. There she dwelled on the edges of the pine forest and tended her garden with lavender-scented breath and honey dripping from her whispering beehive. The crows sat in the treetops basking in the morning sun, gazing down upon her. She smiled on my sight and rushed into her house, bringing out a basket for me to look at. The day was sweet and light, and we sat among the wildflowers as she showed me what she had created. I lifted the lid from the pots of ink and cried out in glee as I dipped a tentative finger into the liquid. "Why, Anika, these are some of the most beautiful inks I have ever seen! The depth of the black, like the gloss of a bird's wing, oh my!" I almost shouted.

"I'm so glad you're pleased! I do believe they are some of my finest work." She smiled bashfully, and I was at a loss of what to say next, so I was grateful when she spoke again. "Would you like to come in? I have a kettle on to boil and a loaf of fresh bread."

"That would be grand," I replied, and I believe that when I stepped through the threshold into her home, I knew in my heart I would not leave.

We fell in love quickly, then, as young folk are wont to do, and I found a quaint home in Pinehollow that I had not expected. I got to know the little rivers, each individual pine, the scent of summer rolling in from the wildflower meadows, and yes, I learned to love the quietude as much as I loved my Anika. Though I was no longer a wandering scribe, I found a bookbinder's workshop in the next village over, and I would copy out pages for the master of it here at our cabin in Pinehollow, walking back along to drop off the completed copies each week with my pack laden with tomes. It was a gentle life, a soft life, and one I enjoyed deeply.

Anika and I wandered often through the woodland, and her skill in inks grew. Soon she was able to make colours I thought impossible, pale lilacs, rich greens and even the brightest yellow I had ever seen. Hand in hand we roamed the hillsides, and I watched as she seemed to float above the clouds, running through the daisy-grass. So free and untamed she was, so wild and wandering. But as time went on and I grew to her know her deeply, I noticed a sadness within her too. Anika laughed often and crowed gleefully to the sunshine, but just as often I found her grey eyes misted over, staring off into the treetops, heartachingly beautiful and melancholy. I wiped the tears from her eyes and held her, but she could not tell me what ailed her heart. The years blended together, mostly with happiness, but although my heart wished for a child, a family to raise of our own, Anika did not fall pregnant. It saddened me deeply, though I did not let her know this, and it was an unspoken strangeness between us. The smallest of things would upset her in an unnatural way. I found one day she had taken an egg from the basket in the kitchen and covered it in a blanket by the fireside. I put it back where it belonged, and when she found it gone and baked into our usual honeycakes, she wailed all night. I could do nothing to console her.

Often I found birds at our window, tip-tapping for scraps of bread and wishing to be inside. At first, I thought it pleasant and to be expected living so close to the forest, but soon it began to irritate me, and I shooed them away, only to find Anika sitting with them in the garden, shooting me dark looks. She drifted further from me and took to sitting outside among the twigs and leaves for hours at a time until the sun set and I would pick her up, frailer than ever, and carry her back into bed.

After a time, she took to vanishing for days on end. At first I was deeply distressed, tearing up the house and running through the forest and hills to try and find her, thinking she had been taken by an animal or gotten lost. So unwell she seemed these days, too thin and only picking at scraps of bread and seeds. After a while I began to expect her absences and she would leave me for days at a time. I loved her deeply still but I was at a loss of how to deal with this melancholy. I often wondered if she was happy with me, if there was another man she disappeared to see. But no happier was she when she returned, eyes still misted over, darker than ever, staring out into the trees. She began to speak less also, squawking strangely when I asked her questions. I thought back on my life as a wandering scribe and wondered if I was fool to have given it up, but when I lay beside my Anika and watched her sleep, tucking the blanket around her tightly, my love-filled heart told me otherwise.

After a while, I noticed that on the days she left me, a crow as glossy and bright as Anika's inks would sit upon the garden wall and watch me as I planted and dug. At first I thought nothing of it, the birds were bold at our cabin, but I began to wonder about it. So curious it was, so unafraid. It would sit and watch me for hours, and as I fed it crusts of bread and fresh fruit, it followed me all the more. When Anika returned from her wanderings that night, there was a light in her eyes that had not been there for a while, and my heart sang to see her so filled with joy. I thought perhaps things could go back to how they used to be, and I dreamed of summer skies and feather pillows that night.

But things could never be the same.

The last time I saw my Anika she wore a cloak of black and wept as she kissed me like it was the first time, before wandering off into the pine woods. I did not stop her. But as I sat outside on the garden bench and watched the end of summer unfurl across the landscape, dripping molten flame in the sunset of early September, something caught my eye. A black figure drifted down over the moorland and the crow came to perch upon my knee. Coal-black feathers and soft grey eyes, staring into my own. I reached a finger out and tentatively stroked the bird, and it closed its eyes and pushed its head further towards me. A wild thing, free, untamed, and unshackled by the human form. I sat with the crow until night fell, and it gazed at me with misted eyes before letting out a caw, flying off into the sky.

And so I bade farewell to my love of flesh and fingertips, knowing her finally content and at peace. And each morning, I awoke to the sound of the crows cawing softly in the dawn sky, and the tip-tap of the blackened beak nudging at the window for my Anika to see me.

LUNE LULLABY

COME, SWEET MOON

AND BATHE ME IN YOUR MILKY WATERS,

FOR THE NIGHT IS YOUNG AND YOUR HALF-SMILE

FILLS THE SKY WITH CHILDLIKE YEARNING.

COME, SWEET MOON

AND KISS THE MEADOWS DRENCHED IN LAVENDER,

FOR SOME SONGS ARE MADE FOR THE DARK,

AND WE HOWL TO YOU TONIGHT IN GENTLE WORSHIP.

COME, SWEET MOON

AND TAKE MY CLUMSY FINGERS IN YOUR CARESS,

SILVER LAUGHTER AND THE PEALING OF BELLS

CARRIES ME BACK HOME TO THE WHIMSY OF THE STARS.

BREATHE IN DUSK
SPEAK IN WORM TONGUE

SNOWDROPS

Drunken cackles and whiskey-soaked breath,

the sky is dark but taxi light blazes in the city.

The moon is shrouded in fog and

revellers call out obscenities

as pounding drums thrum out from neon-lit windows.

But look !

under the moulding bus stop sign,

Spring's first snowdrops,

pushing their way up

through the stale concrete of the city.

8

A TREE'S JOURNEY

First, I felt the tumble of fresh earth closing in around me, rich with the sweetness of spring's first kiss and dusted in fairy breath. I collapsed into darkness and buried my curious head among the soft flesh of the worms, their bodies undulating around me as I nestled deeper into the quietude. April's rain soaked my aching bones and soothed my growing pains with her caress. Under the warmth of gilded sunlight drenching my skin, I pushed upwards and gasped in ecstatic agony, greedily filling my lungs with crisp air crystallised with morning dew. The Sun reached down from his throne and pressed his almighty fingers to my rough skin. With each touch, my layers began to fall away, and I felt the rays of hot breath peeling my skin from its bone.

With a crack, my gangly arms tore free and waved themselves gleefully in the springtime air, knocking side to side like a new-born doe, unsteady in the softness of the breeze. Oh, kingly Sun, please bless me with more liquid gold, pour it molten on me like hot lava and let the sweat of searing rock fall into my gaping ribcage. I drink in the sweetness of fresh rain and giggle as the storm sways me left and right, screaming worship and wishing I would drown on the dewdrops that sparkle, jewel-like on the shards of grass. Taller now, I reach out and press my skin against their soft blades, leaving gentle kisses on them as they dance back and forth and dance in the wind.

Spring turns to summer and I push both upwards towards Master Sun and down into the Mother of all life, the fertile soil, wet and luscious as she births creation eternally. Stronger now, I stand firm in the caress of the wind and feel green buds burst forth from my chest, scanning the skies with new-born eyes and drinking in their first taste of this glorious world. I stand in perfect ecstasy smiling at everyone, sharing jokes with woodland creatures, and giggling with the fair-folk that hide among the leaves. My first summer tasted sweet and ripe, but autumn's magic soon swept me away.

Father Sun visited less, and instead, the sparkle of deep darkness spread over the woodland, dancing through branches and leaving enchantments in her path. A deep sigh of letting go, the trees above me rusted orange and their leaves curled tight. With a shake of their weary heads, they littered the forest floor and rotted in the cold nights. Decay touched a hand to everything in her path, a great shedding, an unburdening, the sweet release of a half-death just waiting to be tasted. I watched in wonder as creatures nestled in the fire-floor and ruddy mushrooms sprung up from untrodden paths. Curious fae uneasy under the heat of the sun now climbed out from gaps in the bark and crawled on all fours, dragging their black bones through dead earth, and whispering ancient magics into the air.

I watched unsure as mighty oak trees closed their tired eyes and exhaled so deeply it echoed through the treetops. I looked around as creatures buried deep and I knew what to do, so I too, let go. A sleep so deep I barely felt the frost as it crusted on my empty branches and winter left his icy kisses on my body. Snowflakes fell and covered the decay in a blanket of starlight, dancing iridescent under the pale moon. My dreams felt like clouds, undulating and drifting like mist in a universe I'd never travelled to before, until I felt the gentle nudge of spring awaken me once more.

Time pushed on, barely a blink in my existence, and I now stood at the top of the forest, smiling down at the seedlings that had at one time been me. My trunk was thick, my bark was rough, and thousands of insects ran all over my body, tickling my arms and finding homes in welcoming crevices. In my branches, nests were built and visited year after year by fat robins and noisy sparrows, arguing over worms and singing their strange incantations every morning. Each of my leaves was so broad and pulled in sunlight, feeding it back down to my roots which ran through the forest floor and made contact with others. I could now sense everything, the toadstools spoke secrets to me, and I felt each movement in the web beneath the earth. I stood connected to every living thing, and I knew them by name, the birds, the creatures that burrow into the earth, the fair-folk living in the spaces between worlds, the spiders that weave intricate webs between my fingers and even the worms that tickled my toes. We were all connected, and we needed each other to thrive.

Aeons passed in this glorious sanctuary, a haven of peace and wild things, but I knew my time was upon me, I had watched many a spring pull up new life, and it was time for me to let go and give them room, let my rotting carcass become a home for life and send my decaying wood into the earth to feed new life. I had dew-tears in my eyes upon that day, brimming with gratitude and the echo of saying goodbye. I stretched to the sky one more time, exhaled so deeply that it rattled the tree-tops and caused the robin to fly from his nest, and let go.

The in-between place of the void carried me gently toward a new life, equipped with the deep inner knowing of my being and the knowledge to pass this to others. In a pool of blood, surrounded by writhing agony and the passion-screams of Mother Creation, my pink flesh struggled free as I gasped my first breath, crying and screaming, placed into unfamiliar hands, I strained my tiny eyes against the darkness, opening them to smiling faces and a mother's eyes glistening with dew-tears of new-born bliss.

9
WHITE RABBIT

I knew they hated me. Since I was a bairn, I had disturbed them deep down to their hollow bird bones. A simple glance or a word stuttered from my thin lips was enough to warrant a kick here and there. I watched often as though I was an onlooker as they coated my body in purple bruises; soft petals of hate. There they were, soft milky skin and golden curls with foxglove pink lips, laughter like the pealing of bells and each movement of their deer limbs so soft and graceful. I remember staring and remarking how even their fingernails were more beautiful than mine, sweet half-moons of white tipping their slender fingers. I felt knife's edge envy at the way their tiny bodies moved, and their eyes lit up when they sang.

Only children we were, but they hated me, nonetheless. They wore pastel dresses with ribbons in their hair, and they hated me from the moment they saw me. Me, with my strange darting eyes and limp hair that fell around me like whispering shadow. The rough grey skin of my dress hung as a dark cloud heaving with thunder, and though I tried to tie ribbons in my hair, the satin always slipped out over my lank strands. I recall watching in despair once as the lilac fabric turned to worms between my fingers. I cast them into the earth and my eyes darted, had anyone seen?

In school I was distracted, constantly staring out of the window into the quivering treetops outside the iron gates. The children played together each day, jumping over twisted rope, and passing around dolls with fleshy skin and vapid eyes glazed over at the sky. No one spoke to me most of the time, so I crept around the back of the building like an alley cat, looking for secrets.

And I found them.

In the spaces between blades of grass, I found tiny villages with toadstool homes and creatures that were barely more than a whisper. I lay in the grey mud and squinted, peering into the hustle and bustle of the goblin market. I watched dreams be bartered for laughter and incantations traded under a black moon. Under fat mushrooms I found my true dwelling place and I crawled under the fleshy stems, resting my weary head and inhaling the ruddy scent of wild places and decay.

I would lie there for hours and often forget to return to my class, instead choosing to watch the flash of a white rabbit as it burrowed into the undergrowth. Sometimes when reclined in half-daydreams, from the corner of my eye I thought I saw a little girl with white hair. She was beautiful, but not like my classmates, instead in a feral and peculiar way. I would see her glassy red eyes staring out at me as she flashed a mischievous smile, but when I turned to look at her, she was gone. I chased her in my dreams, each flash of white pulling me in. Oh, how I searched for her, and how she evaded me, laughing all the while and twitching her nose.

I was scolded when I got back to class, and fingers wagged in my face. I crumbled dried earth from my dress and pulled the twigs from my knotted hair. Teachers in pointed shoes and hair pulled tight into knots shook their heads and shot disapproving looks at one another. Little girls sneered at my appearance and my strange ways.

The years were not kind to me, and life dragged me through its bracken with little care. I grew taller, but not prettier, and was often reminded of this. My dour expression and plain features were not pleasant to look at, and I did not attract anyone who would love me. I recall that I once took all my savings and commissioned a pretty pink dress from a tailor in town, counting down the days until it was ready. I awoke with the sun's yawn the morning it was completed and ran home giddy and lovesick. But as I pulled the lacy fabric over my body, my heart spilled out of me black and blue. Instead of slight and graceful, with folds and undulations where they were supposed to be, I looked lank and lifeless. The bright colour of the dress only served to mock my unruly hair. I looked a beast in a princess gown. I tore it into pieces and threw it into the fire, wailing all the while. I cried until my voice ran hoarse and choking tears were all I could manage. The next morning, I arose, swept out the ashes so they fell upon the dirt, and did not think on it again.

I took on the labour of running a household, rising early to milk the cows and feed the chickens. My heart was weary, and through the tiredness of adult eyes, the blades of grass from my younger years began to close and the whisperings of troll language fell silent. As the days stretched ahead, I cast aside my fancies and did not even glance when I saw a flash of white fur in my vision, until eventually I did not see it at all. I pinned up my hair and cleaned my plain dresses, following the path that was laid out for me. Sometimes when lying in bed, half asleep and half awake, I remembered there was another path through the trees. But it was not my path, I reminded myself. Just the dream of a strange little girl.

By the middle of my life, I was already weary and worn. With body spent and aching, I felt creaks through my bones and my feet were bruised with labour. I had never found anyone to love me, so plain and unsweet, and had spent a life lonesome and bruised. My calloused hands were starting to crack and bleed beneath winter's chill, his harsh embrace. I often wished my life would end and wondered why it had begun at all. A pail of fresh milk, warm from the udder, fell from my rigid hands and I fell to the floor, letting the sweet cream flow into the stone crevices as I lay my head down in the hay. I sobbed then, and let the tears fall, joining the milk and the barn insects as they trotted to and fro.

I lay there for many hours until the night fell and cast strange shadows across the land. Frost crept over the edges of the earth and glistened on the folds of my dress. As my teeth chattered and my bones rattled in my sickly body, I resigned myself to death. Good riddance from a life so lost and unloved.

But it was then that I heard the whispering again.

A strange whispering that seemed to float in from the moors around my home. I brushed the salt from my eyes and stood up, shaking the frost from my skirts. The voice sounded sad and far away, and I wondered if I even knew it at all. I followed the voice up where it became louder until I crossed the boundary from my home and stood on the moors, wading through heather as the last of the wildflower seeds clung to my dress. I inhaled the smell of wild things and felt a familiar inkling in my body. My eyes fell upon something strange then, on the top of the hill lay a small hut with smoke coming from the chimney. Many years I had lived here, and I had never seen this home before.

A tiny tug of my heartstrings urged me forward and led me to the house, and as I pushed the door open, the warmth of a well-tended fire and the scent of spring herbs flourished within my senses. Under the glow of firelight, I set eyes on a maiden so fair it hurt to look at her form, so my drooping eyes collapsed downwards as I stared instead at the floor. She moved towards me silently and set her fingers on my chin, tilting my head towards hers so I could look upon her face. Her white hair fell about her like moonlight and brushed the floor. As my eyes roved her milk white skin, I saw she had tears in the scarlet of her eyes. I moved towards her and reached out silently, aching. But I could not bring myself to touch her.

She spoke now, but it was not aloud. It was a joining of the minds, a whisper through dreams and an utterance through bone. She asked me where I had been all those long years, she was hurt, I could tell. Confusion flooded me, then my memories returned. Memories of a hurt little girl gazing between blades of grass. The white girl, her smile and those red eyes looking at me, laughing in a strange animal language. An ache rippled through my chest I did not think I would recover from; I had let these memories fall from my mind. When she turned away from me, I saw low on her back she bore the tail of a wild rabbit, fluffy and frost-coloured. She took something from the table and turned to present it to me. My hands grasped a rabbit carcass coated in moor-moss. The bones pulsated with warmth and as I touched them, I saw visions of long summer nights on the hillside and fresh blackberry juice coating white fur.

Bones in hand, I pulled her back towards me and I pressed my lips against hers. Her skin gave way under my touch. Too-big bones cracked and fell into the folds of her human skin. Discarded and unnecessary. I burrowed frantically through her flesh and instead of sinew and meat, I saw a rabbit inside, with soft white fur and round red eyes, staring out at me and twitching her nose.

I knew then what must be done. At once I dug my dirty fingernails into my tainted flesh and tore the meat from the bone. Gore dripped from me, but I did not feel it, and so I tore the tendons and muscle away from me. My flesh prison. With a crack I ripped out the human bones that had weighed me down for so many years, and pushed the rabbit bones into the empty spaces, joining my wildness and wilderness.

I crouched down onto all fours and watched dark fur coat my tiny body. My delicate heart beat fast and my eyes adjusted to the world, seeing the magic of hidden spaces and the peace of a wild thing. My white rabbit lover sprung off on her hind legs, leaving the hut with the door ajar. My hind legs sprung forward, and I yipped in glee, lovesick and full of moon longing. I followed her then over the moors, unafraid, burrowing down in the hillside to spend the rest of my days.

10

SLAYER

"There weren't always dragons in the Valley, y'know..." Angren half-whispered into the dense evening air, not to anyone in particular. He sucked on his pipe noisily, the cherry-embers of old tobacco glowing as he gazed out at the mountains surrounding the continent of Vakren.

"Yes, we know. Gods, do you ever tell a different story?" I barked, kneeling down in the dust-covered earth and grabbing one of the rabbit carcasses we'd hunted that day.

"Hmph," he grunted and exhaled slowly, curls of grey pipe smoke weaving their way from his bearded mouth and dancing in front of the mist-thick clouds. I stood up and shuffled from one foot to another, slinging the rabbit over my shoulder and adjusting my pack, the straps were cutting into my skin now and my feet had begun to ache, not that I'd ever tell him that.

"You should have seen it though, Meya. Wildflowers scattered across the fields, the ewes were fat, we had honey every summer, real honey, y'know. You might have even worn a dress in those days. " He let out a half-laugh and began to wheeze, spluttering on the acrid smoke.

"Meya in a dress, now there's something I'd pay to see. No one cares about the damn flowers, Angren, shut up." Kered glanced up from where he was now also kneeling down, busying himself with the rabbit carcasses, his dark hair caught in green eyes as he flashed a cheeky grin my way.

I forced my brows to furrow but looked down as a smile tugged at the corner of my lips, this was the usual order of things. Angren, all muscle and battle scars, bleating on about flowers while we tried to shut him up. I threw the rest of the rabbits over my shoulder, preparing for the descent back into the village from where we were up in the rocky mountains

"There was more to life back then, y'know. More than killing dragons and scrabbling around in the dirt for something to eat," Angren gestured at the carcasses as he spat, yellow and tobacco-stained, onto the ash-coated roack.

"Meya wouldn't know, she's never killed a dragon," Kered teased in a sing-song voice, the man simply lived to antagonise me.

"Believe me, I'm ready for one of those beasts." My fingers absent-mindedly brushed the hilt of my sword, I'd been training for that kill my whole life, I thirsted for it.

"Ah, she's young. I didn't kill my first until I was twenty one, she'll get her chance," Angren grunted.

Kered snapped back, "Time's running out, only a few weeks until you're twenty one."

“Shut up,” The words spilled from my mouth before I could stop them, though I knew he would tease me more if he knew his jokes were getting to me. Though I was used to his jests, I felt a flare of anger rise up in me, this one stung a bit. It was true, it was our job to protect our village in any way we could, and everyone else had slain a dragon, except me. It’s not like I didn’t want to, those foul creatures had crawled out of the shadow when the continent of Vakren first fell into darkness and I couldn’t wait to feel my sword tearing into one, I just hadn’t been given the opportunity yet.

I followed Angren’s mournful gaze and looked out at the valley myself; most of the villages were now abandoned and razed to the ground, mere ash and dust from what used to be a bustling market town.

“Ah, you’re just kids. But it was dark days, let me tell you. First the crop began to fail, then we noticed a strange disease on the trees, that was when those foul things arrived from the far reaches of the world. In the beginning, it was only four-legged beasts and we hunted them well, but then the dragons came,” he swallowed and tapped his pipe on a boulder that sat next to us on the rocky outcrop and grey ash fell to the floor, joining the rest of the dust left by dragon fire and destruction.

“We saw it in the sky first, a peculiar shadow fell upon the village... the first dragon,” he spat. “We shot at it, wounded it, and it set the forests ablaze. Sheep turned to ash before our eyes and burnt bodies lay in the streets. It was dark days indeed, and the days that followed since haven’t been much brighter, we won’t have peace until we rid the land of those foul beasts... Pshh, you’re right. I’ll shut up.”

Kered and I shared a glance as Angren grabbed his pack off the floor and started on ahead of us, beginning the journey back down the mountain pass. Grey skies, that's all it ever seemed to be anymore. The mountainsides that were once lush and green were now home to singed forests, charred bone and malformed, molten rock. We arrived at the village as the sun began to set over the hillside, bathing the leaden scenery in a sickly orange light. I imagined the glow of the first blaze that killed so many, destroyed so much, and although the night was warm, a shiver ran down my spine.

"Evening, folks. Was gettin' worried when I didn't see you come back 'fore sunset. I've heard whisperings that a Silver Drake is about," Callon, the blacksmith chattered away, setting his tools down for the night.

A Silver Drake. My heart thrummed in my chest as I remembered Angren telling me of these beasts, milky white scales, blood-red eyes, and able to unleash an inferno so deadly that they could obliterate anything in their path, whether stone, metal, or flesh. Silver Drakes were responsible for half of the bloody destruction in Vakren.

"There's always damn whisperings, half of them amount to nothing, don't believe everything you hear," Angren huffed.

"I'm telling ya, folks seen it wandering in the wood, best to keep away," Callon urged.

"If you say so, Cal. Night." Kered threw a rabbit to the blacksmith and he nodded in appreciation.

We set our weapons down by the door of our tiny home and busied ourselves with skinning and preparing the rabbits for a stew, putting the tasteless meal on to boil in a pot above the fireplace. Not many of us still had family alive after all the attacks, so we lived in haphazard villages and shared homes with one another made of what wood could be salvaged, prepared to move and rebuild at a moment's notice.

We were Dragon Slayers by trade, I had just finished my training, and there were only three of us left alive to protect the village now. Angren was getting old, he had passed on his knowledge and it would soon be time for us to do the same to others who were willing. Kered often poked fun at me for being the only woman he'd ever known who wanted to fight back and do something about these wicked beasts, and I took the teasing because I knew I couldn't be the only one out there in the world, it was just a matter of getting out of this dump and finding others.

The world wasn't always like this, perhaps it could be like it once was, a place where things grow and darkness was confined only to those putrid corners of the world, it had to have come from somewhere, maybe it could go back there... I was dying to get out of Vakren and find a place that hadn't tasted dragon fire, maybe see one of these flowers that Angren was always going about it, find people more like me... I was torn out from my daydream by an almighty bang at the door, causing me to splash the boiling stew on my lap and yelp from the scorching heat as I leapt up at the unwelcome intrusion.

"Who the hell is that?" Kered raised his eyebrow and looked over at the source of the sound, I shrugged and glanced over at Angren who frowned and made his way to the door.

Pulling the door open, a tiny figure stood doubled over, shaking uncontrollably. It was Alys from the village, a delicate little thing, but she'd always been kind to me. Angren pulled her into the house and sat her down on a wooden stool by the fire as her body was wracked with breathless sobs.

"Calm down Alys... what is going on?"

"Its taken him... its taken my boy... that beast!" she shook and wailed, her mousy hair a mess under her hood, looking like a waif of a thing between Angren's thick muscled arms.

"Tell us what happened."

"We were out behind the house, he was playing like he always does, I turned around and he was gone! I heard there's a Silver Drake about, please... he's only three years old!"

We glanced at each other and although I felt for her, I had to stop myself from rolling my eyes, old Callon was spreading dangerous rumours and getting all of the village in a fluster. It was almost impossible that a Silver Drake had taken the boy, but if it had, there was no way he was still alive. Angren looked into her doe eyes, pale blue and brimming with tears.

"We'll search for him, Alys. Please just stay here inside the house, we'll be back by sunrise," she nodded and buried her face in her hands as he turned to face us. "Let's start with the woods."

Kered grabbed his sword, tying his belt around his waist and grabbing his cloak from where it hund next to the door as I followed suit and reached for my weapons. I looked at Alys and patted her on the shoulder as I left our home, offering the only thing I could think of.

"Feel free to eat the stew..."

I never was a good comforter.

. . .

We split up and agreed to search different areas of the charred woodland. What should have been fear turned to a burning excitement deep in the pit of my stomach, if there really was a Silver Drake in the woods, this was my chance to prove myself to everyone, to show them that I was capable of slaying a dragon.

Silently and with steely resolve, I made up my mind, I would be the one to find and kill the Silver Drake, if there even was such a thing around. The night air was calm now, and the moon and stars shone a pale milky light across the blackened earth. I darted between the wizened trees and moved at pace, the forest was a good size, and it would take me a few hours to get into its depths, but I was used to tracking and no stranger to being out in the woods for hours, so the time flew by as I searched between the trees for any sign of noise or movement. I was so focused on that dragon, looking for a flash of white, that I almost missed the child before me, wandering in the deep dark of the woods.

Alys' little boy was plodding through the bushes ahead of me without a care in the world, babbling nonsense to the charred trees, the lad hadn't even realised he was so far from home. I cursed under my breath and exhaled in relief, of course he hadn't been taken by a damn dragon. Alys probably took her eye off him for far too long and he wandered off. I shook my head as I moved quietly towards him in the distance, not wanting to scare him on my approach, but as I stepped forwards my feet stopped abruptly and I stifled a gasp, he had walked into a bear's nest. In the middle of the clearing, a bear cub rolled on its back among the dry grass.

Oh gods, its mother must be close by.

. . .

I scanned the area, squinting in the thick of darkness and pushed forwards towards the child, unsheathing my sword from its holster and grasping it firmly between both hands, on guard.

As I approached the clearing, the mother bear clambered out from between the blackened bushes, spotting the unwelcome visitor making his way excitedly towards her cub. My heart thundered in my chest and my breath quickened as I began to run now, watching in horror as she threw herself up on her back legs and let out an almighty roar. I was so close now, just a few metres away from the clearing, when a peculiar moon-shadow fell upon the earth, followed by a flash of white in the corner of my eye, causing me to freeze, as if fixed to the earth.

The bear stumbled back as the Silver Drake landed on the earth, causing the branches to tremble and a thud to echo throughout the forest. For a split second I had half a thought that it was smaller than I had imagined, now it stood before me and raised itself up at the bear who roared back in protection of her cub. With a sweep of its talons, it reached for Alys' child, grasping him between its claws as he began to wail in confusion. It turned slowly to face the bear and let out a sound like nothing I'd never heard before. It was a deep, unearthly roar, stirring something deep inside me that felt like it had lain dormant for a long time. The bear yelped, grabbed its cub in its mouth and leapt into the bushes. Then the Silver Drake turned to face me.

Milk-white moonlight glinted off the silver of my sword as I raised it up towards the creature, attempting to hide my trembling arms as it stared back at me, my blade only inches away from its face. With shaking breath I stood before the beast, and my fear turned to wonder, I doubted if anyone had been this close to a Silver Drake before, and if they had, they wouldn't be alive to tell the tale. Its scales were so white they were almost pearlescent in the starlight, gentle lilacs and pastel blue danced under the light of the waning moon. Its eyes were indeed red, a deep scarlet that bored into my very soul and made me feel weak at the knees. As I stood with the metal of my blade so close to the beast, I felt something shift within me. It stood before me now, able to obliterate me in a matter of seconds, tear out my innards, incinerate me where I stood, and yet, somehow it only looked sad. Its crimson eyes stared back at me and its long snout was soft, almost feminine looking.

I felt my life's purpose fall out from under me as I gazed upon it, everything I had been taught and trained for swirled in my mind. With an ache in my chest I was hit with the dull realisation that I couldn't kill the creature. My fingers slowly unfurled and I let my sword clang to the forest floor, staggering back a few steps. It reached out with its talon curled around the child who was now wailing and afraid, and placed him softly into my arms, where I held him tight as he buried his curl-covered head into my chest and sobbed. The Silver Drake bowed its head to me as I reached out with trembling hand, feeling sparks throughout my body at the electric that danced between us as my fingers made contact with its cool skin. It closed its eyes and let out a long, slow breath, then turned away and flew off silently into the night sky, leaving me standing, babe in arms, breathless, confused, and with a strange sense of heartbreak.

Wolf-Eyed

Hot blood dribbles from my gums again.

I spit fire-froth and pollute the earth,

the lightning-tang of iron in my mouth still sour.

Blood-matted fur wet and viscid from the kill,

tiny bones crunch and contort beneath me,

mangled tendons and sinew catching in my teeth

as the muscle deforms betwixt my iron jaws.

I hear the rip, then a twig-crack echoes.

Movement dances in the mist-dense thicket,

storm-eyes dart, pricked ears twitch,

paws tangle thorns and worms beneath.

Muscles ripple, I am a phantom, crouching,

blood dripping, awaiting another dawn.

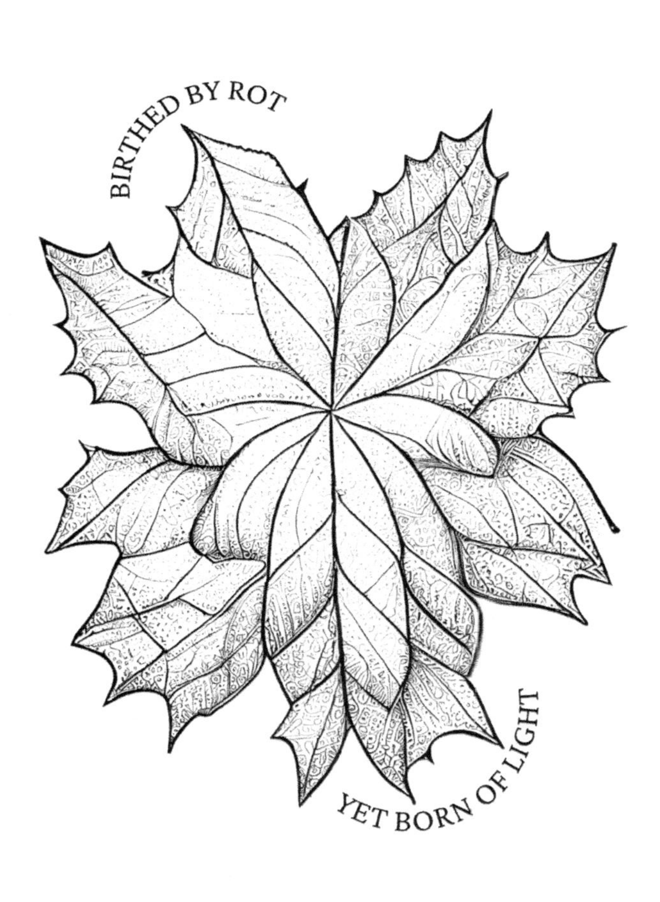
BIRTHED BY ROT
YET BORN OF LIGHT

More Tree Than Person

Soft moss begins to form in the crook of my bark-skinned arm,

so I bury my muddy toes deeper into the decay-kissed waters of the bog.

My cheeks splinter and my spiderweb hair tangles in thorn-studded branches,

so I howl as I offer my pleading hands up to the tear-filled sky.

Tiny spring buds begin to form on each fingertip and laugh as they unfurl under the sun's gentle caress,

so I close my eyes and return home.

11
WISP

Goddamn it, I forgot the tent pegs.

I threw my bag to the floor and exhaled through my teeth. After driving four hours to get here, this is not what I needed. My mate, Peter, looked up from the backpack he was rooting through and rolled his eyes at me when I told him of my mistake. Jack, he told me, you had one job - bring the tent, including what we need to put it up! I wasn't exactly an expert hiker, but I thought I'd be able to manage that at least. We'd been here five minutes and already I was wishing we'd planned something else for Peter's birthday. I told him I was sure I could find some twigs or something, hammer them into the mud. Sorted, right? He muttered something about it not exactly working that way, but I shook my head and made my way to the edge of the forest anyway.

Wild camping up in Scotland had seemed like a great idea at the time. Just us blokes, a campfire, a few beers, and the serenity of the great outdoors... or something like that. I'd never really understood why freezing to death while being eaten by midges was a holiday, but Peter was adamant that this was what he wanted to do for his birthday, and who was I to deny a man I'd been best mates with since I was about six years old.

So here I was, laden with waterproofs I'd bought just the day before at Mountain Warehouse and the old tent I had from music festivals when I was younger. I chuckled at the sights that tent had seen, more than one or two cans of beer, that's for sure. I almost left it there along with our camping chairs and rubbish like everyone else did, but it wasn't cheap, and I didn't want to have to just buy a new one again. I hadn't even thought to check if the tent pegs were still there. After a day of driving, we'd arrived at the campsite, if you could call it that. A field surrounded by hills with trees at the bottom, more like, it didn't even have a proper toilet or shower. Talk about being out in the sticks... I made my way into the woodland at the edge of the grass and began scanning the ground for twigs. I knelt down and picked one up, only for it to snap between my fingers and turn to wet mush. Goddamn it, this was going to be a nightmare.

There was no path in this wild woodland, so I struggled my way through the bracken and dead leaves, batting midges away as they tried to bite me. Even the birds were irritating here, tweeting away and singing about God knows what, it sounded like they were enjoying my misery. I took a big knife with me and hacked at the plants as I walked through, they seemed determined to get in my way, but not with this machete they wouldn't. It was satisfying to watch the blade slice through the greenery and clear a path for me. I needed to get out of this place and get back to Peter so I could crack open a beer and get a steak on that barbecue, I would feel better then. My fingers were freezing now, and I wished I brought gloves, rifling through the frost-coated forest floor looking for twigs was not exactly what I planned to do with my weekend, but I knew we needed somewhere at least half-warm to sleep, and I didn't want the tent to blow away in the night. An ugly little spider dropped from God knows where and landed on my jacket, causing me to shout out in alarm before laughing at myself and what a little girl I was acting like. I needed to man up. I squashed it against my jacket and brushed it away, ugly little creature.

As I was kneeling down, poking in the mud for the sturdiest sticks I could find, my eyes were drawn into the thick of the forest, and I spotted something strange in the distance. I couldn't quite focus on it, but it looked at first glance like someone else was walking in the woods, flashing their torch. I stood up now, the hairs prickling on the back of my neck, and squinted out into the darkness. I spoke aloud, asking who was there, and an uneasiness settled in my stomach. What was I playing at? Scared of shadows. I needed to sort it out if we were staying here all weekend. I shook my head and looked away, but no, there it was... a strange light flickering in the distance. As I stared up ahead, I thought about fireflies, but they didn't live here, did they? Maybe it was some other weird insect. All sorts of creepy crawlies in these parts. As I tried to move closer, it floated further away, and I couldn't quite reach it.

I set my pile of twigs down for a moment and picked up my pace as I moved through the woodland. For some reason, I just had to find out what this thing was. It was annoying me now, that I couldn't see it properly or understand it. I wanted to know. My feet sank into the mud, these cheap boots were not properly waterproof, and though ice-cold water soaked through my socks, I kept moving. I felt weird, a bit sick, maybe I had eaten something bad, or I was hungry. I should probably turn away and just get back to Peter.

Peter. The tent. I had almost forgotten why I had come here in the first place, what was I doing? I turned back and scanned the ground for the twigs I had gathered, but I couldn't find them in the mass of leaves and stupid plants on the forest floor. Exasperated, I decided to just pick a couple up on the way back and that would have to do, I didn't want to wander here any longer. But as I turned to leave, I felt the strange sensation grow stronger, as if an unseen force pulled me to look behind and see the strange glowing orb dancing in the distance. I tried to pull away, but my feet seemed to have a mind of their own, carrying me through the woods to chase after this light. My heartbeat quickened as I felt cold sweat slick my skin, I pulled at the zip of my jacket, suddenly I felt hot, constricted. Where was this damned light coming from?

I followed it through the woods, though each time I took a step, it moved further from me. Bramble tore at my trousers and nicked my skin, I felt the heat of the cuts forming on my hands, but I was distracted by this light. I had to find it. I pushed onwards, deeper into the tree. The sun had almost set now, and there was no light to guide me, save for this orb up ahead. Time seemed to slow, and the minutes blurred into one another, how long had I been gone? Had I heard Peter calling for me, or was it simply my imagination? I shook the thoughts away and pressed on, ignoring the ache of my muscles, and slipping into some kind of trance. The orb danced before me, weaving its way through the branches, illuminating the leaves, and mocking me as it moved out of my reach. I stretched my fingers towards it, grasping, clutching, but each time I opened my hand, there was nothing there. Irate, I let out a whine into the night air, why couldn't I find the light?

My head felt hazy, like I'd been up all night drinking cheap vodka, and for half a second I wondered if I had been. I staggered forwards and felt I would burst into tears. What was I doing? Where was I? An orange light began to glow at the edge of the horizon, could that be dawn already? Yes. The sun was rising now, pulling me out of the trance of night-time. My fingers snapped in the air, the last attempt to find the light... but then, it was gone. Under the sickly sunrise, the blanket of night had been pulled from the trees, and the orb was gone. With a sick shudder, I thought of Peter and the tent. Dread filled my body as I scanned around the woods and realised I was completely and utterly lost. Had I been drugged? What was I playing at?! I couldn't see the way back to the campsite. My feet began to sink into the grey mud, and I realised just how cold I was. Teeth chattering, my bloodied hands grasped upwards, clawing at branches to keep me from sinking deeper into the bog, but they snapped off in my grasp and left me gasping, screaming.

I watched a swarm approach and let out a wail, midges covered my exposed body, and I batted them away, smearing their tiny dead bodies into my skin. Spiders crawled on my face and rushed into my ears, my eyes, my mouth. Even the vines and plant stems wound their way around me as I yelled and thrashed against my demise. Bog stench soaked my senses as I screamed for Peter and howled to the sunrise, but no one came. Deeper I sank, and strength began to leave me.

As I inhaled the grey rot of the quagmire and felt consciousness fade from my body, I saw in my mind's eye, a strange creature holding a lantern, waggling his finger at me in disapproval.

Inside it, playful and mocking, danced a silver-white orb.

12
HONEY

I do not know how much time had elapsed, only that I had forgotten the taste of honey.

Honey. Dripping lovesick from the comb like molten gold. I had lived through long summer days and dreams scented with raspberry seeds and butterfly wings. I had been licked by the swollen sun and splashed my toes into clear water for fish to suckle upon. I was a child of the heat and light, a lover of salt-sweat and burning orange skies. And in those long summer days, I always had my honey. The bees knew me by name. They felt the ground quake on my approach and saw the ripples of sunlight following my feet. My stubby fingers found crevices in old bark and carried me higher into the treetops where I reached, giddy, into hives and my hand emerged dripping in stolen syrup. I lapped up the liquid gold from the comb and felt it run down my face. Sticky and wet, I basked in its sweetness, I did not mind the tack of it clinging to my clothes.

But it was dark now. And the dark was flavourless. And I had forgotten the taste of honey.

I gaze up at the ink-well sky and my heart shatters like careless footfalls upon an ice-tainted lake. A single tear rolls down my fleshy cheek, and I catch it upon my finger and press it to my lips, whispering prayers to the old gods and new. But it is not sweet and golden, it is dark and bitter. I wail then for some time. How long for, I cannot say, only that the noise which came from me was an animal noise I had not heard before, perhaps akin to a species long since passed from this world. I wail until grit scars my throat and my voice disappears into the black ether. I feel embarrassed then, and my beady eyes dart to see if anyone had seen my outburst. But there was no one there. Of course, there was no one there. I had wandered these tar-pit mountains for many moon cycles now, there was never anyone there.

The howling of wind through the jet stone should not have been comforting, and yet oddly, the sound was soothing to me. Despite the bitter chill of the ice whip against my bare flesh, and the deep ache of my muscle sinew, the lullaby of the song through the rock holds me for a moment. I let myself daydream of long summer days searching for beehives and honeysuckle. Was it a mere second, or had hours passed? I feel a semblance of peace.

Then, an image in my mind, a hound bigger than any I had seen before stood before me dark and heaving, syrup dripping from his jaws. My skin rattles. The peace was gone. And so returned the darkness. That shadowed pit in the crevices of my hollow bones and the recesses of my belly. I press onwards through the tunnels, urging my legs to take another step forward as the soles of my feet burn blackened against the callous ground.

For a moment, I struggle to recall why I am there at all, or even any of my memories. But they filter through the quagmire of rotten thought slowly, and I clutch onto them for a moment before the inky darkness of the endless chasm creeps over me and enters my mind. I cannot not seem to recall my purpose. Why did I leave the sun? Where was my honey?

Yet still, I continue.

Following one winding passageway after another, the tunnels seem an infinite chaos with no discernible pattern and no layout I can figure out, each doorway promising the end and yet leading to another shrouded tunnel. It is mostly silent, save for the occasional flurry of bats, the endless drip of water falling from the high ceiling above, and the echo of my footfalls on vast stone.

Pitter patter.

I join the steps of insects with pincers and one hundred eyes as they scuttle along the jagged floor. Sometimes, I try to play with them, to chase them and dance as they do, but even they won't have me. They run into crevices where they know I cannot follow and look back out at me with those eyes glinting. They're mocking me, I know it. There comes that shame again. Even the beasts will not sit with me.

Beasts. Ah yes, the hound. As I rambled the wild woods, I took a fancy to a hive. Lovesick I stalked it, pining for it, singing sweet things to it, waiting for my moment. The wolfdog had stolen the honeycomb of my desires from my very grip and led me to this evil place in chase. I am coming, honey. I am coming. Should I howl to him now? A rotten weight presses down on me, causing my steps to become soft and slow. How did I think I could ever keep up with those insects? I lie down for a while and let shadow overcome me. I cannot see the moon nor her milky light, and I do not know the hour. I think for a moment, considering abandoning my life and hope.

Then. There it is. Honey, is that you? A golden light glows in the distance, promising an end at last to the vast tunnel. Oh honey, could that be you? Sweet nectar of heaven, you have come to save me from this place. Invigorated with a fool's hope, I scramble towards the doorway and heave the stone pass until it shifts.

There are cracks in the ceiling here and the moon's milky light wanders in. I reach out and drag my pointed tongue against her, but silver is cold and reserved, and so she shies away and looks at me with disgust. She knows I am a creature of gold and honey. Rusted leaves have blown in from the entrance and litter the floor, soaked in rainwater and moisture from the cave walls, filling the room with the sweet smell of natural decay. And something else... the musk of a beast's fur, wet dog dripping from the cavern walls. I move towards it. The beast lies in the corner of the cave, warming himself against the crackle of the fire, gilded honeycomb set between his paws. My heart races. He sees me and spreads his lips, his fanged smile sharp and expectant. I crouch down on my haunches, feral, lustful, and slink towards him, I am coming for my honey. His head snaps to the side, I follow by instinct.

Something else, how could I have missed it? To the other side of the fire sits a figure, and as I approach, I see the wiry grey of their hair, cascading endlessly across the cave floor. The firelight flickers against the walls, illuminating the figure, and I see her clearly now. There she sits, atop a wooden stool, with a loom before her. The loom is so vast that her arms seem to stretch impossibly long as she glides the thread under, and through, and up, and across. The cave is black, but her tapestry is vibrant. Hues I had not set my simple eyes upon before. Hues of impossible sea indigo, sunrise orange, a white so pure I look away, bashful. She turns to me and smiles, her face cracked and weary, but her eyes light and sparkling. I follow her gaze back to the loom and there I see it all. Within the loom, I see a thousand lives unfold. It shimmers one way, then another, and if I soften my gaze, I see before me a newborn infant, the shadow of a yawn, fingerprints undulating into mountain ranges, and the seed of a secret. She's almost finished her masterwork, her frail fingers glide the final piece through, and I bear witness all the while, tears brimming my eyes. She sits back and smiles now; her work is complete.

The hound sits up, stretches, and yawns, drawing me from my stupour. Over he pads, nonchalant, leaving the honeycomb by his bed, and catches a dew claw on the thread of the masterpiece. Horror quakes my being, existence itself falls away and I am lost in the whirlpool. The thread unfurls, unwinds, the windows of the earth close as I feel my life ending. I look to the old woman and tried to scream, but it comes out as birdsong and the pealing of bells. Gasping, tears collapse from me. She simply smiles, then takes my hands – ice cold – in hers, and I feel a rush. The warmth of ancestry.

"My child, are you ready to give up your honey?" She speaks in a voice of a thousand people, the tumbling of a stream and the emptiness of the void.

As she stares at me, I see bone dust forming in the cracks on her face, flakes of skin begin to fall away, and the light dims from her eyes. I know she will leave us soon. I glance over at the honey lying golden and sweet on the stone floor, abandoned by the hound. I can hear it sing to me now, the seduction of the saccharine. But I understand now, there are duties and mysteries of more importance than earthly ignorance and desire. My heart aches and begs me to say no, but instead, I nod. The wolfdog howls, a glint in his eye as he laps up the syrup and the nectar pours down his throat. The old woman smiles, is she my mother? Grandmother? Or both and neither? She guides my hand to the spool and sets it upon the loom. I have never weaved before, but I know just what to do. I pick up the loose threads and my fingers find their way, guided by the song of my ancestors and the women who weaved before me. I watch as my grandmother-sister falls away, her bones crumbling to tomb dust and snowflakes, swept away in the rushing wind of the tunnel.

And so, I begin the spiral dance. I am left to the eternal duty. I weep as I feel the flourish of thread, weaving the fabric of this life until the next.

13
WELL-DWELLER

"I told you to stop looking down that well." My brother's voice was strained, and he exhaled through his teeth as I tore my eyes away from its black abyss.

I glanced up at him, towering above me in his too-big overalls, all sandy hair and wild brown eyes. I shifted on my feet and picked at the skin on my nail. He had, of course, told me this many times. And each time I ignored him.

"I told you to stop looking. What if you had fallen and left me all alone? It's no job for a child. Get inside." He shook his weary head and pointed towards our cottage.

His rebuke was rooted in care but still it filled me with a seething rage. A sharp sort of venom that bubbled under my skin and made me want to hit him. But I didn't.

Instead, I scampered inside at his behest, slamming the door to the cottage and letting that anger spill down my face as hot tears. I wiped them fiercely with my sleeve, he would not see me cry. It was just us now, and I had to be brave. Father had left us before I was born and now Mother was gone too, though he would not tell me when she would be back. I sometimes wondered if she would return at all, but I was too afraid to ask. Sickly light filtered in through a slit in the curtain, though it was not enough to illuminate the stone walls. Mother had always kept it clean and light, leaving crushed lavender on the windowsills and each room flowing with fresh air. It even seemed lighter when she was here, humming old songs and baking rosewater biscuits. But now it was just my brother, only seventeen years old. He could hunt for rabbits and chop wood, but he did not know about leaving lavender on the windowsill, or fresh flowers on a vase on the kitchen table.

And he was allowed to fetch water from the well, but I was not.

We didn't speak much that night and ate our meal in silence together. He still helped me brush my hair, though he pulled on the knots more than I was used to, and he tucked me into bed too tightly. He left an unsure kiss on my forehead, and I wondered if he meant it. Summer days slowly collapsed into autumn, and the leaves were starting to blaze on the trees in the forest when I spoke my weary thoughts aloud, "Will mother come back?"

He only looked at me and patted a hand on my head. I did not know what it meant.

I sat on the grass outside and picked the last of the summer daisies. My mother always braided them together in the most wondrous way and set them in a crown upon my brow, but though I sat in fierce concentration, I could not seem to get it to work. Frustration tingling at my fingertips, I threw the daisies to the ground and wept, burning tears of injustice and confusion. I tried to help my brother with work around our home, but I was never any good at any of it. I dropped the pails, wasting good milk, and didn't have the strength to chop wood for the fire. I went to bed feeling ashamed most nights, and I whispered for my mother into the darkness before I slept, "*Where are you?*"

If I am honest, I often watched my brother collecting water from the well. It was only a simple circle of stone, but the dark recesses of it whispered gentle lullabies to me. It was as though it called to me in a language no one else could hear. I felt jealousy fester inside me like a deep pit. Eternally unsatiated. Why shouldn't I gather water too? Why should he keep the well all to himself? What started as a seed in my belly grew roots and took up through me until it turned to branches budding with resentment.

As the years passed, I grew taller, and my mother never did return. I did not expect her to come now, I did not stand at the garden gate to watch for her golden hair. I did not whisper to her in the blanket of night, and I did not ask my brother about her again. I was older now, stronger, and I like to think a little wiser also, yet I was still not permitted to fetch water from the well. My brother told me it was no job for a girl, that only he was to do it. He began to spend more time away from the cottage, venturing into the nearby town under the pretence of selling butter and cream. I knew he mainly visited the town to talk to pretty girls, and I also knew he was too poor for any of them to take a real interest, and so I quietly pitied him for it.

I was tall enough now that I did not have to climb to look inside the well. I could simply rest my hands on its cool stone and gaze down into the urging blackness. You could not see to the bottom, but if you were quiet, you could almost hear the rushing of its water down in the fathomless depths. I pondered for a while. It was a fine summer's day, the sun shone high in the sky, and I'd busied myself with gathering sweet berries and darning the never-ending holes in my brother's clothes. But he was not here today, and I suppose we did need water for the house, didn't we? Why shouldn't *I* fetch it instead? Surely now I am strong enough to do it, tall enough and clever enough.

Excitement rattled through me, and I felt my heartbeat quicken as I took the wooden pail to the well. I ran my hands over the stone and exhaled into the moss that coated the outside. *Hello well.* My trembling hands secured the pail with a rope before gently releasing it into the pit. Glee wracked me in a way I had not thought possible, coursing through my blood, and I urged it further and further down, willing it to splash and reach the water. Go, go, go! Almost there now, but wait -

As I gazed into its depths, I thought I saw something that did not belong, though I did not recognise its shape. Had an animal become trapped? Taller I was, but still slight, and so I climbed onto the rope and slowly lowered myself down into the well. It smelled of cold water and wet moss on rock, and suddenly, I was afraid. But down I went, deeper and deeper into the darkness. The air caught in my throat, and I almost cried aloud as I saw what I had been searching for. Two beetle eyes glistened from the shadow, catching on what little light filtered down this far. A shudder ran through me, and I dared not speak. Perhaps I could climb back up, quickly, quietly...

A voice sounded from the well, rough and dry as a death rattle."Hello there, little one. You can see me? You can hear me?"

Trembling, I tried to speak but it came out only as a whisper. "Yes... Who are you? What are you doing here?"

Was I going to die like this? The creature moved out from the darkness, and I could see them now, a squat sort of shape, around half the height of myself, perched on a shard of stone, jutting out from the well's wall. Their skin was rough and grey, their hair wiry, and they wore brown cap, jacket, and trousers, though they were riddled with holes and stains.

The crackling voice sounded again. "I am the household spirit. Once I dwelled by the hearth in your home, not many of you still possess the sight to see me as I am."

My head throbbed and I could scarcely utter my next words. "And what are you doing down here?"

The creature came forth, further into the light, and I saw how sickly he looked, how weak. He spoke again. "When I dwelled in the house I was given oats and milk, and respect was awarded to me, and so I gave in return. But soon, all forgot about me, and I had not the strength to stay in the house anymore. I found this cool, quiet place, and I decided to stay here awhile. You do look very much like her."

"Like who?!" Panic flooded me. "My mother? Did you kill her?! Is she dead?!"

He removed his cap slowly, revealing a bald spot in the middle of his wiry hair, and pressed it to his chest as he looked down sadly. "Yes, she is dead. No, I did not kill her. Your mother found me here. She took pity on me and brought me treats, lowering them down into the darkness, but so starved was I, that it would not satiate. She told me she knew of the older, more powerful sustenance, of pressing her blood to me and feeding me in this way. So, she climbed the rope down into the well but fell and hit her head. She died here. I am sorry."

I felt my heart shatter, though an arrow had pierced my chest, winded and wounded. I had no words for this news.

The spirit continued, "She died here, and I sang to her as she passed on. Do not worry for her soul little one, she is with us all now, even now, I see her. Your brother found her here and buried her in the woods."

I wept then for some time. I had known for a while deep down that she was never coming back, but now it was real. I felt betrayed that my brother didn't feel he could tell me of her death, but I understood his worries about the well. When I took my head from my hands, the creature still stood, black eyes staring out at me. He looked so frail, so cold and abandoned. I took pity on him then and asked, "Are you going to die too?"

"Perhaps. Though I am not sure I can die, maybe I will simply fade from this place. Go somewhere else... but I did very much like it here. I enjoyed the rose petal biscuits most of all."

My heart felt splintered, and I dragged my palm against the edge of the rock until it tore my flesh, pouring blood down my arm. I reached for the creature, and pressed it to his skin, watching him gasp. His little face flushed with colour immediately, from a sickly grey to a rich brown, sweet and fresh like crumbling earth. All at once, the holes in his jacket and hat were mended, and his hair became thick and lush. Tears brimmed in my eyes again, but he pressed a warm hand to my cheek and brushed them away. I crawled up from the well with bloodied hands, and he followed me silently. He smiled as the sunlight hit his complexion, and sighed a long, patient breath.

I turned to him now and spoke, "Come inside please, spirit, and take a seat at our table. You are welcome in this home, and I shall keep you fed all the days of my life."

And so, the spirit took up his rightful place by hearth of the home. He was left a share of milk and oats, and as he grew stronger, he used his ways to send blessings over the land. The calves grew fat, and the milk flowed from their mother. The herb garden sang in aroma, and the now-fertile soil bore a bounty so great, we never went hungry and had plenty to sell. My brother married a kind woman and built a home for them next to the cottage.

As for me, I tended to the land in reverence of all the spirits who dwelled there. I left lavender on the windowsills, sang to the household spirit, and indulged in many rosewater biscuits.

COMPASSION

THEY CALLED HER WEAK FOR NOT SLAYING THE DRAGON.

WHAT ABOUT GEORGE? SIGURD? CADMUS?

ONE BY ONE THEY RAISED THEIR BARBAROUS WEAPONS AND GOUGED A GAPING WOUND INTO HIS GLORIOUS NECK,

SCALES OF STARLIGHT DISCARDED, MAGIC-SOAKED BONES SOLD FOR PROFIT AND DAGGER-TEETH PARADED IN A WICKED BOAST.

WHAT A PITY, SHE IS NOT STRONG ENOUGH TO DO IT.

LET ME TELL YOU INSTEAD HOW SHE BEFRIENDED THE DRAGON,

SENT HIM DEEP INTO THE MOUNTAINS TO HIDE FROM THE SWORD,

HOW SHE LAYS GENTLE FINGERS ON THOSE IRIDESCENT SCALES AND STARES INTO THE VAST GALAXIES OF HIS ANCIENT EYES.

THERE IS WEAKNESS IN THE SIMPLICITY OF DESTRUCTION,

AND STRENGTH ETERNAL IN COMPASSION.

ROOTS GO DEEP

She Has the Sight

She has the sight, they say, like an old country witch.

She lies back in the meadows and squints,

seeing the worlds that exist between blades of grass,

gone when the breeze knocks them back together.

She is not pretty, no one would call her that.

Her face is plain, her laugh too loud, and her footsteps too heavy.

She whispers over fox bones and gathers strange plants in

the pockets of her dress as she dances.

She sings to the wildflowers and laughs at their jokes,

visiting secret places between the cracked bark of old trees.

14
MOTHER-EARTH

First, I hear their footsteps dance. Betwixt clumps of dense, black earth and perpetual worm tunnels, the melody veers through the undergrowth until it reaches my dormant ears. Quiet, they try to be, but their tiptoes reverberate through the sodden ground as loud a wolf cub cries for its mother. Tentative, they are. Not knowing they need not be.

After aeons, they still understand nothing about my ways. They tread above my mossy coffin and deliberate among themselves, bickering and nickering like horses half-starved. I almost laugh, but instead I only smile. A curving of my cracked bark lips which creaks in the undergrowth and causes black beetles to scurry towards the surface.

In their lives, generations pass, though for me it was nought but a soft blink of my spider lashes. Now the ritual begins. How charming that they still call upon me in such a way. Do they not know they need but sigh onto soft breezes or whisper secrets in the ear of a badger for me to heed them?

Let me tell you something.

What if I told you the way was simple?

Yes, you can carve butterfly-leg incisions upon your flesh and weave in the peacock's feathers of verdant oak leaf and honey. He will not miss them. Yes, you can reach into the fecundity of the earth's rot and smear its ancient symbols upon your form. Of course, you can pound the drum of deer skin until your palms bloody and howl to the blackened sky.

If you like, you can even lay out the offerings one by one; a crow's claw, the needle of a holly leaf and secrets carved onto hare bones. You can whisper incantations over them as you work and let the death-lullabies collapse into the earth. It's true, I will hear.

But listen to me, child, that is not the only way.

What if I told you this, instead. When the sun king rises next morn, come rest awhile upon the brow of the hill and watch the lovers of night and day pass one another. Press a fox's ear to dawn's dew and you shall hear me there. In the tickling of a spider's leg or the sigh of wind upon the moors, you shall hear me.

Take your mangled fingers and press them to the bark of a beech tree. Watch as your blood runs smooth against her flesh, she will not mind. Stay with her in those early hours, the quiet moments when the sun yawns, and let your tears flow. Howl your woes into the woodland. She will not mind.

And I will be there, and I will not mind.

15
LAMBTON WORM

First, I am swaddled in sticky blackness and the stench of putrid bog water. I am contented, comfortable, and the rot holds me in its arms. I rest my weary head in the inky dark and taste sweet decay on my lips as carrion slips beneath the languid depths into my mighty jaws. How wondrous, these thousand years of peace. Serenity. At home in the place where I belong.

Then. All at once. Clawed up into fire. Searing sunlight that burns through closed lids and inflames my icy flesh. Writhing and dying. Hot flesh taut and cracking and mouth gaping and whining and screaming no words into the sickly silence. I see his face, my captor. Resentment is birthed.

Plunged back into icy depths, moss-sludge settles into the burning crevices and soothes my wounds. I breathe again. Growing pains begin to strike. A dull ache that travels through muscle sinew and leaves a hollow pit in my bile-soaked stomach.

Straining against damp rock, scraping my beautiful scales. I, made for vast waters, expand unwillingly in the space I don't belong. I gaze up at the midnight blue sky splattered with stars and feel my heart breaking.

Heavy rocks crack and tremble and shatter beneath my mighty touch. I can taste the cool air of freedom and move towards the silver jewels that beckon above. The feel of night air caressing my scales like soft kisses, a blanket of grass and freshly turned earth writing with fleshy pink worms.

A sound travels on the midnight breeze and wafts towards me. A soft bleating, unfamiliar, followed by wisps of thick white wool. Then. A flash of red. Hunger burns within me and suddenly hot warmth spills from my lips, the taste of mangled flesh so sweet.

Something changes. A quickening of my heartbeat and a sickening in my stomach. Writhing and turning inside my body, organs pounding and grinding and gnawing with the abyss of hunger. Rosy cheeks, a sweet face, devoured.

But a fullness too, and peace. The first peace I've known since I was free. It's good, yes, it satisfies. And so, night after night I crawl through the streets and stalk their young. I hear their screams, but I cannot stop. They are my prey, and I am oh-so-hungry. Without the carrion of the sea, in this place I don't belong, I am ravenous. Unendingly ravenous. Terror spills onto their faces and I drink in the horror, feasting on their anguish.

My body grows strong now, without the confines of my prison. I walk in peace, killing and destroying, and rest awhile on the hill. My tail hugs the dew-tipped grass and indents it with my majesty. All is well.

Then he returns. That man.

The same fingers that plucked me from peace to a land that burns and hates and is not mine. I despise and detest. I know they conspire with one another. He stalks, he seeks, around every corner he is waiting for me. I can see him even in my dreamless sleep. He is coming.

Silver steel rings and lunges towards me, I look up at the night sky. I think of bog waters glittering under starlight, the sweetness of decay. I do not move aside from his attack. Take me away from this place I do not belong. The blade breaks my flesh and I taste the edges of sweet oblivion.

Please, take me home.

16

A TROLL'S PROMISE

"You must wed." My father's voice echoed through the throne room, reverberating across the stone walls.

There was an emptiness that lingered in this place, making the noise of his speech jarring in the silence. It was not empty in the way of quietude and peace, the feeling found at the bottom of a sweet tea when only the dregs remain. And not empty in the way of the gentle quietude of winter's first snow fall, but empty as pitch. The long night waiting at winter's gate, the hollow feeling in the pit of your belly when hunger sits there too long. This was an emptiness of grief and bog rot, of stolen crop and a pillaged home.

I paced the stone room, my footfalls loud and the hem of my dress scraping along the floor. I shivered at the words and the room, this room always ran cold despite the tapestries lining the walls. The fire that once blazed had been snuffed and dwindled to embers. Why did he never see fit to light it?

He spoke again. "Daughter. Do you not listen to me? You must wed."

I countered him now, quietly. “I heard you father. But you know I do not wish it. What man could make me happy?”

My brother snorted, he knew my words were folly, but I could not blindly acquiesce.

“Daughter, why do you trouble me so? Your happiness matters to me, this you know, but you must be wed. You are old enough now and it should have been arranged already. I will see that it is a good match.”

My heart sank. “Father, please, do not make me do this.”

“As princess it is your duty to wed. you must do this.” His voice was stern now.

I dropped to my knees before him, begging. “Father, I am not cattle to be sold off. Have I no say in the matter?”

He looked upon my face, and I knew he saw my late mother there which swayed his reasoning. He set his head in his hands and his voice was almost a whisper when he spoke. “Very well. You are permitted to have one requirement of your suitor.”

My heart soared but I kept my gaze soft, underestimation was the strongest weapon. I knew what he expected of me, handsome young men with soft curls and muscles. Land, riches and beautiful dresses. I needed to play this carefully, so tears brimmed my doe-eyes as I asked, “Do I have your word on this matter, father?”

Impatience tinged his voice as he called out, “Yes, you have my word. Now speak it.”

I spoke louder now, my voice carrying. “I will go with the one who presents me with the most beautiful thing in the world.”

He exhaled and I knew it was a sigh of relief, pretty necklaces and rare flowers were easily found for rich lords. A smile spread across his face as he replied, "You are the princess, I believe that is fair. But when you are presented with the most beautiful thing in the world, you must go with the one who brought it to you, I shall hear no quarrel on this."

"Yes father. I will go with the one who presents me with the most beautiful thing in the world, that is my promise." I do believe my smile was even wider than his, for I knew they would all fail.

Word was sent far and wide across the kingdoms, and suitors began to journey to us to present their hand. My father did not like it, but men both wealthy and poor lined up to claim me, each bringing with them the most beautiful thing they could find. I sat upon a chair and watched as each of them climbed the stairs, and I took audience with every single one. My brother rolled his eyes at my spoilt behaviour, but I only smiled sweetly. Muscled men with soft golden skin and long brown curls came to me, presenting me with yellow jewels found buried in the sand from their distant lands of sunshine, only to be turned away and return again with wondrous silks in impossible shades of pink and purple. Rough men with work-tarred hands came to me, presenting jewellery made by their expert skills, silver and delicate as the stars of the night sky. Diamonds as large as my fist were placed upon soft cushions and set into my lap for me to marvel at. Jewellery, riches, and finery beyond measure.

I turned them all away.

My father simmered with rage, but he could not take back his promise, and so word spread that these riches were not enough for me. Men came to me then bearing all manner of strange things, claiming they had found the most beautiful thing in the world. Parchment with the deed to huge palaces by the sea, strange herbs that made you lovesick and gleeful, and even fair maidens bound in shackles, slender and shiny haired, doe eyes brimming with tears.

But when the lord of the High Tower came to me, something in the set of his jaw and the wild desire in his eyes instilled fear in my heart. He stood there robed in gold with jewels dripping from his throat and set his offerings down to me, purring with gentle words. "My lady. The most beautiful princess, I pale upon the sight of your beauty. I have come to offer you the most beautiful thing in the world, everything I own."

And so, he sat with me, and unfurled the maps of his excessive lands to the East. He presented me with flowers and grain, of strong pale horses, of maps of his wealth and the servants of his tower. I shook my head at all of it, and resentment flickered in his eyes.

"What will this princess need to be content? Name it," he growled.

I smiled sweetly, but my heartbeat quickened as I replied, "I shall be presented with the most beautiful thing in the world."

Anger flared up in him, but he stepped away and bowed. "Then you shall have it."

He sent riders to every corner of the realm to search for the most beautiful thing, and each of them returned empty-handed. Bitterness took over him and my father grew impatient, but he was a man of honour, and could not break his word. The lord did not return for some time, and I hoped he had given up the quest, but my brother assured me differently. A rider had returned with news of great wealth to the North, immeasurable riches that lie in the mountains of the troll king.

A shiver ran down my spine, and I wondered if I had taken this too far. Yes, regrettably, blood was spilled on my account. For that I am ashamed. For many weeks, war was waged upon the troll mountain. A place of secrets and magic, not to be trifled with by the petty desires of men. I watched the sea rolling in and out from my tower and shed a tear then. I hoped in bitterness the lord would not return, that he would die at sea and be smashed against the rocks.

But return he did.

The door of the throne room banged open one morning, and the lord's guard spilled into the room. The lord came before me, death shining in his eyes as he began, "My lady, I have done what you asked of me. I have found the most beautiful thing in the world, and I present it to you now."

His guard dragged something forward, a figure shackled and beaten. He pulled the sack from his head, and the troll king stood before me. Bog-coloured skin, hairy ears, twisted features and black eyes heavy with woe.

The lord spoke again. "I present you with all the riches of my land, all the riches of the troll mountain, and his magic to use at any time we desire. There is nothing of more value in the entire world."

He laughed but it was bitter. He thought he had won for certain.

I kept my silence and simply shook my head to the lord. He snapped then, and pounced towards the thrones, my father's guard leaping before me.

Rage tumbled from him as he roared, "Liar! She lies! The princess lies! Nothing will be enough for her!"

My father looked sickened, and fury filled his eyes also.

The troll king fell to his knees before me, bound in shackles. He offered his empty hands up and spoke with a voice of husk. "My lady, I heard that you have given your word to go with the one who presents you with the most beautiful thing in the world. Is this true?"

"Yes." My voice was almost a whisper.

"Here I present to you the most beautiful thing in the world: a choice, for this is what all women desire most of all. And now you must go with me, as you promised. But in my kingdom, you shall be free, if you wish to marry me, I will take you as my wife, but if you tell me no, you shall live in peace. What will you say?"

My heart soared at the wisdom and courage of him, and I took his shackled hands in my own as I wept. "Troll king, you have presented me with the most beautiful thing in the world. And for this I shall marry you, so good of heart you are."

Never have I seen such white-hot fury surround a man, and the lord took his sword to my troll king, but it shattered into a thousand pieces before it touched him. The troll king set a manacled hand upon him, and there he transformed into a squealing pig, nipping at our ankles.

My father looked at me with heartbreak and pride in his eyes, I had kept my word and assured my own happiness, and so I took the hand of the troll king. The shackles fell away from him, and we journeyed back to the mountain on the breath of a feather. The men fell away easily upon the news their commander now walked on all fours and rolled in the mud, and we enjoyed the days of peace and freedom together.

TREE FOLK

Ten gnarled fingers tip tap - crack -

withered bark creaks and ferns unfurl.

In the deep crevices, damp moss forms

and wildflowers nod where hair should be.

Mud caked lips and grit and dirt,

a friend to worms and all that crawls.

Lightning cracks in the shadow of the oak,

a gnome-home, an owl's lair, a secret door.

Gnarled fingers tip-tap and worm their way in,

bare-bones snatch at feathers and dust.

Wolf-walker, fox-stalker, tree-creeper, chest-beater,

howl as wind through quivering branches,

feral-eyed night-stalker, gone by morn.

SEASICK HEARTSICK
UNBELONGING

Legacy

The hanged-god looks downwards and laughs.

It spills from his cracked lips and bursts from his belly,

A dank cavern of carrion and decay.

It's a bitter smell, dragon-bile and rotten fruit,

But it carries well on hot air and permeates the rock.

Eons pass but the stench remains.

It lingers in dark places, the spaces between secrets

And promises trampled into black mud.

17
SALT

The sun had not yet risen over the cliff's jagged edge when the strange light first came into my room. It started dim, as all light does, a mere thought, nought but a whim in the distance, but it grew to a pale gold that filled the little room, pouring in like molten honey through the windows. It invited itself in and made itself comfortable in the cobwebbed corners, illuminating the peeling window frames and the tiny wooden bed with its duck-egg blue blankets, tucking itself in for the night.

The light weaved its way around the room, looping and curling through cracks and crevices until it reached my slumbering form. I exhaled softly as it rested awhile atop my eyelashes, coating the edges with silver like spring's last frost. Clinging. Desperate. As the light pressed itself against my sleeping eyelids, urging me to awaken, I was torn from my crab-claw dreams, so I rubbed the sea salt from my eyes and made my way to the window. I pushed it open softly, letting in the cool breeze, and gazed out at the rolling sea, lovesick with no lover.

There, squinting out into the darkness, I saw it.

On the far side of the shell-speckled beach, the gaping mouth of a cave I had not seen before was bathed in a white light. I'd spent more than a lifetime in this little town, I knew the undulations of the shore, the sound of the waves lapping the sand and I knew the caves like the back of my hand. I had spent my days of youth splashing through them, chittering with gulls, stealing the rotten fish from their beaks.

But never had I seen this cave before.

I pulled on a thick cloak and pushed open the heavy wooden door to my cottage, the sharp scent of saltwater and seaweed filling my senses, the crash of the waves against white relentless as always. Tonight, the air had a taste to it like nothing I'd experienced before. There was salt there, yes, but as I breathed in the icy swell of midnight, I could taste the silver milk of the moon and her gentle caress as she lay naked in fullness, bathing the black ocean in her sweet-tasting light.

I made my way down the cobbled pathway to the shore, my seashell teeth chattering in the tang of the night cold. My fleshy toes felt unfamiliar as I sank into the sand, approaching that white light that called to me so

At last, I stood at the mouth of the cave.

In the light, I could see colours fade in and out, unlike any I had set my eyes on before. In the haze of it, I could see fish scales and squid ink, and hear strange music, as though spindly bones twanged discordantly. The light ushered me gently into the dark recesses of the cave, and in the centre, I saw a hooded figure, tending to a fire of pure white light. I watched as they pushed driftwood into the flames and burnt incense upon it that gave off the sharp tang of brine and shark eggs. The fire gave off no heat, just light, and as I stood there, I thought for a moment that I could hear a woman's voice, singing sadly over the rattle of fish bones. The hooded figure beckoned me over and I turned to face them now.

A woman stood there, grey skin drooping from her face, her hands calloused and blackened. Where her eyes should have been were gaping voids instead, and I couldn't help but stare into their abyss. Her skin was cracked and coated in dusty coral and a decaying starfish clung to her bare breast as she sang an ancient sea shanty to the white light of the fire. Her flesh was so dry that as I watched, it began to fall away from her. I reached out to try and help, wishing I could coat her pallid complexion with blubber and whale-fat, but as I moved closer, I realised now that the cloak over her shoulders was in fact grey skin covered in soft velvet hairs, shrivelled, and dried. It smelt of seal flesh and brine. The scent brought sea-tears to my eyes, and they began to spill onto the sand, crystallising and becoming part of the seashore.

A shiver ran through my rattling bones and as I reached out to pull my cloak tighter, I found that it was also made of the same cracked seal skin. I cried out and the wail that came from me was an animal voice that I could barely remember was mine. The woman lunged towards me, grabbing my trembling hand, pulling me over the fire, and forcing me to stare into the abyss of her cavernous eyes.

As I stared, I saw many things. First, I saw the gentle lull of the tide, pooling behind her gaze and spilling out from those empty sockets onto the floor of the cave. Then, I saw myself in another life. I felt my blubber fat and soft, a tiny pup with soft white fur and eyes like black seashells, dancing under the depths. I saw myself lying on the cool beach, laughing with my sisters as we stepped out of our skin and danced naked under the light of the mother moon. I tasted her then as I do now.

I saw my gaze follow the village, its tiny houses, and its peculiar people. I watched myself join the mundanity one step at a time, overcome with puppy curiosity. I took the rough hands of a man and then watched him leave, closer to the sea than I could now ever get. I drank the bitter wine and smoked the cigarettes and shivered in the cottage alone, night after night, aching for something I had forgotten. My skin festered in a dark cupboard under the stairs, cracked and moth-eaten. I felt my own heart break like falling cliff rock and sadness spill into my seasick bones. I saw loss and boredom, hate and bitterness. I tasted the sorrow of an outsider.

By the time I had remembered, my seal skin had rotted and dried. With each step I took further from my nature, each distraction, each mind-numbing activity that dampened my spirits, the skin had begun to crack. I felt the cloak around my shoulders tighten and begin to restrict me, breath would not enter my lungs. Dark blood caught in my veins and coursed through my aching false body.

I tore it from my shoulders and cried out, pushing into the water that pooled in the bottom of the cave, begging it to become soft once more, but it would not moisten. Panicked, I sobbed to the woman, grabbing her hand, shaking her, but she crumbled into a thousand tiny crabs before my eyes, and I watched and wept with envy as they returned to the sea. I tore at my soft human suit and wailed for my sisters and my lost self. More laughter, more movement, more connection, the kiss of salt spray and ocean waves. I had denied myself of my nature for aeons, and it was all but lost.

I knew what was needed, but was I too late?

18
FURY FORGED

He was angry now; it was the third time I had asked.

The first time I asked him I had stood there as a child, soft of heart and gilded in flower-petalled innocence. Child, he first told me, think of kinder things, and go bury yourself in daisies. He shook his head and even laughed back then at the fanciful thoughts of a little girl. Misguided, but harmless. I was ablaze in those days, eyes brimming with wonder and a friend of bees. I spoke to the ants and whispered my secrets to trees; I was free and alive, and the scent of the sweet air filled my little lungs with joy. I sought him out for his skill, and I had taken my question to him in full hope, expectant like springtime buds. At this rejection, I took his dismissal home with me, and it seemed even as I walked, the scent of flowers had dimmed. I strained my ears. I could still hear the speech of bees but it had quietened just a little. I tried not to worry, he had told me to think of kinder things, so I would.

I retreated to my life and back to my duties. I was too old to be running around like that anymore, they said, so they plied me into whale-boned dresses that squeezed my growing ribcage so that I could not run across the heathered moors. I stayed mostly indoors from then on and learned my letters and numbers as I was told. Often, I saw him, and I tried to catch his eyes, but he did not see. Was he avoiding me? I brushed it from my mind. When I took turns in the grounds with the other young ladies, I smiled serenely as I remarked upon how beautiful the flowerbeds were, but batted away the insects that came toward me on their quest for pollen.

The second time I asked him, I was older.

I had begun to widen; my rosy cheeks were soft and flush, and I laughed under the blossom of apple trees. They told me to hush and be quiet. To sit up properly, to pin back my hair and speak softly of proper things only when asked of me. I bundled myself in swathes of heavy fabric and felt my fire begin to flicker. When a man first put his cold hands on my skin I barely shuddered, instead I smiled sweetly and closed my eyes. But I felt a candle flame twinge deep in my belly and it almost awoke the blaze that used to lie there. I gazed through the window at the summertime bees, and half of a memory came to me of their chatter, or was it just a dream?

I ventured from my home to the workshop where he spent his days. Bent over, banging metal, and feasting on sparks, he looked out at me from a smoke-smothered face, the soot not quite reaching into the creases that lined his skin. He remembered the joke and even deigned to chuckle, a smile spread upon his features, but it did not reach his eyes. He batted a hand towards me, told me he was working, and this was no place for a lady. Look, he said, your dress is already blackened from the workshop floor, away with you. And so I went, with a strange empty longing taking root in my heart.

The third time I asked, I was a woman grown.

Full and aching, I stood before the old man with his fires blazing in front of him and asked once more with a woe-gilded voice, "Will you forge me a sword?"

He looked up from his work with his brow all-a-furrow and set his hammer down with a heavy clang. He did not find it funny this time.

I could see the irritation lined plain in his face. He spat on the ground next to his anvil and shook his finger at me, rage seething. I was mocking, he thought, and I could feel his white-hot anger. It was improper, he said, for a woman to speak of such things. I was a few years past my prime now, and the flutter of my lashes no longer caused them to smile and say sweet words to me. I was worthless and spent, and without my youthful sway, they would not listen to me. Dismissal, disrespect, and unworthiness had nestled so deeply into my bones, I knew I would have to be remade. My life-bruised skin cried out, burning with the fires of the forge, and I craved the vengeance of cold steel in my hands more than ever.

I wanted to cry out, shriek, keen, press his wrinkled face into the pit of the forge. But instead, I smiled, and I buried my anger. Life rolled on, the village swelled, and industry grew, and eventually the blacksmith died of old age. I stood by his graveside mostly unfeeling, only a semblance of pity in my heart. After that, the smithy became unused, unnecessary now with the new methods of creation. I felt akin to it in that way, and often I dreamed of its fire smothering me, rushing her molten waves over my skin. My hair was pepper-speckled now, and my bones creaked when I walked, heavy with the rot and malcontent of an ill-conceived life.

Night terrors took me often, and I felt my mind begin to weary. My time was almost up. I heard death knocking at my door, felt the icy hand upon my shoulder. "Just one more night," I said aloud into the night air. Give me one more night. With my waking eyes I saw embers, and I knew they whispered to me. I tore from my bed, joints aching, and picked the lock on the rusted smithy door, the rotten wood giving way more easily than expected.

And yes, there it was.

A small fire burning in the centre of the workshop, embers crackling on coal. Ah, my love, there you are. I tossed kindling upon her and shrieked in glee as she roared upwards, inviting. I rifled through discarded metal and took a slab of steel between tongs, dipping it into the flames. Sickly yellow drenched the blade, and I took it to the anvil, the little strength I had left in my fading body hammering down upon the metal to form the flattened point of the blade. Sweat fell from me in release and my chest heaved, my breaths crackling in the heat of the workshop. I set a hilt upon the blade and stared upon it, lovesick and giddy.

If you will not listen to me, you will not help me, you will not allow me to be who I am, I shall simply do it myself.

I gripped the white-hot blade in my hands and felt its power flow into me like dripping honeycomb. How sweet, my love, how right it felt. A shock of ice - a brush of death upon my cheek with those unworldly fingers. Yes, I am coming now, I am coming. I held my blade tight and leapt upon the fire, her flames licked my skin and I felt it fall away. The stench of burnt hair filled the workshop and I cackled all the while. I felt the pressure, the pain, the dismissal, the rage, all fall away from me.

And as heat seared through my sinew and I took one last breath before hurtling into the safety of death's embrace, I do believe I heard the chatter of bumblebees from out of the window, telling tales of springtime flowers, and the promise of good pollen that was to come.

OFF-BEAT (FINAL THOUGHTS)

Listen to me, I never wanted the same things as they do.

I want to bury my ugly toes in soft mud and howl to the moon and stars for all to hear. I want to cackle too loudly and bare my big teeth and stalk the fox back to her lair.

I crave the way the sea looks black at night and the spaces unspoken between words that reveal the most ancient of secrets.

I want to tear my best dress on the bracken and knot my hair with the spikes of hawthorn, smear my cheeks with the juice of the berries and declare war.

Give me peat-whiskey and unfinished playlists and bad singing in the shower. I surrender to the blackbird's first song at dawn and the glint in his eye like he has a tale to tell.

I want to build my own nest of twigs and feathers and lay down and wait for worms to fall into my gaping mouth.

OFF-BEAT (FINAL THOUGHTS)

I RUN TO THE DANK PLACES WHERE MUSHROOMS THRIVE AND INSECTS COMMUNE, I LISTEN TO THEIR SONGS AND LAUGH AS THEY TICKLE MY HAIRY LEGS.

GIVE ME IMPERFECTION AND SAVAGERY, LET ME LEARN DEAD LANGUAGES BY CANDLELIGHT JUST TO FORGET THEM BY MORNING.

I NEVER WANTED THE SAME THINGS AS THEY DO, *AND THAT'S JUST FINE.*

ABOUT THE AUTHOR

L. Morton has been writing stories since she could hold a pen and stapled together her first ever homemade 'books' as a young child.

Drawn to the ancient magic of traditional folktales and mythology, she believes in the power of storytelling to change the world. Oaken Tongue is her debut publication.

www.leodruneshoppe.com

instagram.com/lunaleodrune